Shifters by the sea

Includes: Taken by Him & Bared to Him

APRIL 2025
SPUNKY GIRL PUBLISHING
Canada

Also by Jan Springer

Cowboys Online : Moose Ranch
Cowboys for Christmas
Cowboys In Her Pocket
Loving Her Cowboys
Cowboys in Her Heart
Always Her Cowboys
Claiming Her Cowboys

Intimate Secrets
Intimate Lover
Intimate Kisses
Intimate Stranger

Kidnap Fantasies
Jade's Fantasy
Zero To Sexy
Christmas Lovers

Perfect
Perfect
Imperfect

Pleasure Bound
A Hero's Welcome

A Hero Escapes
A Hero Betrayed
A Hero's Kiss
A Hero Wanted
Captive Heroes

Pleasure Bound Boxed Set
Pleasure Bound : COMPLETE SERIES SciFi Erotic Romance Boxed
Set

Tentacles Shifter Erotic Romance
Taken by Him

The Desperadoes
The Pleasure Girl
In Her Bed
Awakening Eve
Dark Solar

The Key Club
A Merry Menage Christmas
Sophie's Menage
Jewel's Menage
Jaxie's Menage

The Outlaw Lovers
Jude Outlaw
The Claiming
Colter's Revenge
Tyler's Woman
Resistance
The Outlaw Lovers
Alpha Outlaws Boxed Set

Vampira
Sweet Heat
Dark Heat
Wet Heat
Crimson Heat

Standalone
A Touch of Menage
Naughty Girl Desires Boxed Set
Nice Girl Naughty
Sinderella Sexy
The Biker and The Bride
The Fire Within
Bared to Him
Pleasure Bound : A Futuristic Adult Romance Boxed Set
Merry Menage Kisses Boxed Set
Inner Girl Rising
Stripped Naked
Risqué Girl Delights Boxed Set

A Holiday Menage
Ménage À Trois
A Hitman for Hannah
Billionaire Boyfriend
Edible Delights
Vampira
Toygasm
The Dark Side

Watch for more at www.janspringer.com.

Shifters by The Sea

A Two Book Bundle
Jan Springer
Jan Springer dives into the naughty world of tentacle
shifters...human by day and shifter by night, these primal
males will claim their mate...in more ways than one.

Taken by Him
Tentacle shifter Calder Croft catches the female's scent when
she passes his California marina, and he can't ignore the way
she fires his blood. After meeting her, he's stunned to
discover Cat has no idea she's a shifter about to come into
her Change. It takes all his self-control to keep from taking
the sexy woman right on the spot.
Tattoo artist Catalina Brown falls head-over-tattoos for the
stranger who asks for a tentacle tattoo on his...most sensitive
body part. Normally, mixing business with pleasure isn't her
thing, but he's a sensual magnet she can't resist, particularly
after she experiences a wicked-hot artistic high while
tattooing his every succulent inch.

Calder has to tell Cat the truth about her heritage. Will she accept her birthright as a shifter—or succumb to madness, forever losing their chance at love?

Bared to Him

Human by day and a tentacle shape shifter by night, Gray Wagner, is the last male that Alaskan custom boat maker Miranda Bolton dreams of falling in love with. He's irritating, arrogant and teases her to no end. Due to her ancestry, Miranda knows she has a good chance at becoming a shifter just like Gray. Alone with him, traveling the high seas on a yacht, she unexpectedly can't stop fantasizing about him. Suddenly Gray becomes the only one she wants to mate with, and she's going to make sure she gets what she wants...

Gray Wagner promised Miranda's dad that he would keep his daughter safe during their week-long ocean voyage to attend a mutual friend's wedding in California, but Miranda's succulent scent is driving Gray wild. He knows he shouldn't be thinking about doing all the dirty and delicious things he wants to do to her, but all his promises to Miranda's father disintegrate when Miranda shifts and Gray goes primal...

Collections

Other collections by Jan Springer include Her Sexy Cowboys, Intimate Secrets, Dark Solar, Risque Girl Delights, Shades of Ménage, Pleasure Bound, Naughty Girl Desires, Alpha Outlaws, A Touch of Ménage, Shifters by the Sea, Vampira, and Merry Menage Kisses.

Copyright

License Notes

This book is permitted for your personal use only.

All Rights Reserved

Author Note

This is a work of fiction. Characters, places, settings, and events presented in this book are purely of the author's imagination and bear no resemblance to any actual person, living or dead or to any actual events, places, and/or settings.

Taken By Him

A Tentacles Shifter Erotic Romance ~ Book One
Jan Springer

Tattoo artist Catalina Brown falls head-over-tattoos for the stranger who asks for a tentacle tattoo on his...most *sensitive* body part. Normally, mixing business with pleasure isn't her thing, but he's a sensual magnet she's instantly attracted to, particularly after she experiences a wicked-hot artistic high while tattooing his every succulent inch.

Tentacle shifter Calder Croft catches the female's scent when she passes his California marina, and he can't ignore the way she fires his blood. After meeting her, he's stunned to discover Cat has no idea she's a shifter about to come into her Change. It takes all his self-control to keep from taking the sexy woman right on the spot.

Calder has to tell Cat the truth about her heritage. Will she accept her birthright as a shifter—or succumb to madness, forever losing their chance at love?

Chapter One

"**H**e wants you to tattoo his *what*?" Catalina Brown's good friend Misty Rivers shrieked in shocked laughter. They sat at the picnic table outside Catalina's trailer, in the private RV site she'd leased for the month, just south of Carlsbad, California.

"His entire cock," Cat said plainly as she set down her wineglass. She enjoyed how Misty's face flared a deep red that matched the "By The Sea Tattoo Parlor" decaled on the side of Cat's nearby fifth wheel travel trailer.

Her friend's brown eyes gleamed with excitement. She slapped her tanned hands onto the picnic table and leaned forward, shaking her head in denial. "No way."

"Yes, way."

"You're not seriously considering doing *that*?" Her friend shook her head again with increasing excitement. The mane of her shoulder-length, chestnut hair flew wild in the warm, late-afternoon, July breeze that drifted off the ocean behind them.

Catalina answered with a casual shrug of her shoulders. Truthfully, she wasn't sure she could actually do what this guy had requested. The only reason she was considering tattooing him was because she loved the design he'd emailed to her. It looked challenging and she loved a challenge.

"I'm meeting with him first thing in the morning. He wants me to make it so an octopus is tattooed across his abdomen and belly, with tentacles reaching around his waist, down his legs, up around his nipples, one around his back, and he wants his cock to look like a tentacle."

Misty laughed. "Well, he certainly found the right woman for that, didn't he? You've always loved drawing sea animals and tentacles are your fetish. I mean, look at your website. The gallery is loaded with images of sea tattoos you've done on your clients."

A warm glow flooded Catalina at her friend's praise. Cat came through this town several times a year to visit with her old high school friend-turned-actress. It was always a nice treat to see her. But yeah, Misty was right. Cat never turned down tattoo requests that had to do with seahorses, octopi, coral reefs and especially tentacles. Truth be told, tentacles turned her on so much she couldn't even have a normal relationship with a man because she was consumed by the fetish. When men found out she needed tentacles surrounding her when she had sex, they dumped her like a hot potato.

"But having his entire cock tattooed like a tentacle. I mean, ouch!" Misty grimaced. "That would hurt, wouldn't it? I mean sensitive parts and all."

"It would hurt nine times more if I used the machine. I'll do the bamboo technique on him instead. Small needles, less pain, more color, less blood, and I can do what he wants with the bamboo method nine times quicker because there's a faster healing time. So, pain will be at a minimum."

Misty scrunched up her face. "Okay, quit the boring talk about the mechanics behind how you do your tattoos. What I want to know is, how will you handle tattooing his entire cock and abdomen and all the rest he wants done? I mean won't you be embarrassed when you do that *intimate* part?"

Totally.

"Why should I be?" Catalina lied. "Customer satisfaction is my goal, right?"

Besides, she was dying to see how good of an artist she could be in such a unique area of a man's body. Sure, she'd tattooed cocks before, but never an entire one and never one that swept off the man's stomach and onto his...appendage.

"You're a tentacle nut, woman." Misty laughed and nodded to the side of Catalina's forty-five-foot-long trailer. The walls had been decaled in dark, ocean blue with white-capped waves and a variety of sea life designs swirling on all four sides. The biggest drawings, of course, were the sexy tentacles with suction cups. Her business name and website URL had been boldly brushed in red on all sides of the trailer too, in order to get free advertising as she drove along the highways.

The trailer she pulled around with her bright-blue pickup truck was her world. She ate in it. Slept in it. Worked in it. Traveled in it. She'd been travelling up and down the Eastern, Western and Southern United States Seaboards for five of her twenty-three years, always drawn to stay near the ocean. Heck, she'd loved the ocean ever since she could remember, and had been creating sea life pictures ever since her mother had stuck a crayon in her hand.

That love for ocean animals had naturally followed when, at the tender age of sixteen, she'd become, much to her parent's annoyance and disappointment, an apprentice to a tattoo artist in her hometown of what she called Boringsville, Oregon. When her mom had passed away due to colon cancer, her dad had hooked up with the local slut and married her. Catalina had learned quickly she was in the way of the newlyweds and, at eighteen, she'd packed up her bags and headed for the coastlines, working at enough tattoo parlors to learn virtually everything she needed to know about tattooing. She'd never looked back.

"I don't know about this guy. He sounds kind of creepy, getting a tattoo like that." Misty frowned, but Catalina just couldn't get into the maybe-this-guy-was-dangerous mode her friend's face was showing.

This man actually sounded intriguing, and she wanted to meet him. Big-time.

After Misty left, Catalina headed back inside her trailer and quickly popped the email from her mystery client up on her laptop. She read it over for the hundredth time since getting it a couple of days ago.

Would you be interested in doing this design on me? I've heard you are an expert with certain aspects of sea life.

Then he'd asked if she would do an octopus on his belly and the tentacle thing. Yes, he had to have a fetish or something. She also loved how he seemed to be a passionate romantic, because he wanted a red rose entangling a rusty, metal-shaped lock with a heart-shaped keyhole, dangling from the tentacle that wound around to his backside. Kind of like a surprise for the woman he would present himself too. Lucky girl.

Catalina smiled and, against her better judgment, found herself getting turned on at the idea of guy wearing such a unique tattoo. Something like that would be exactly what she would tat on her own man.

Immediately, she shook those thoughts away. No romance in her life. She was perfectly happy doing the travelling tattoo gig. She'd put a lot of money in setting up her business and she had all the proper sterilizing equipment and work licenses required by each state she visited. She wouldn't give that up for anybody. Even for a fantasy of a client who wanted a tentacle tattoo.

PROMPTLY AT NINE THE next morning, a knock rattled her side door. He was here! Suddenly Catalina was all flustered and nervous. Second thoughts about this man whirled through her head. What if he *was* a madman like Misty had said? No, he couldn't be crazy. He was into tentacles, just like her. And she wasn't certifiable.

Blowing out a tense breath, she cast one last look into the bathroom mirror. *Perfect.* She looked great. Professionally dressed in loose jeans, a white blouse and, of course, her dangling, tentacle earrings. Not that she was trying to make an impression on him or anything.

She grinned in the mirror, took a second to pinch her cheeks to make them look a bit redder, thus healthier. The knock came again, and she left her tiny bathroom located near the back of the trailer and hurried down the narrow hallway to let him in. As she swung the door outward, she couldn't help but inhale at the tall, clean-cut, dark-haired man who looked up at her with the greenest eyes she'd ever seen.

"Hi!" he said and then smiled. A dimple exploded on his left cheek, and she swore she forgot who she was and why he was here. For a very long split second it seemed as if only the two of them existed in the world.

"Am I too early?" he asked in a very deep voice, and she realized she'd been staring at him.

It was nine a.m. sharp, and he already had a nice five o'clock shadow lining his cheeks, strong chin, and the area over his upper lip. And he had the most kissable-looking lips she'd ever seen.

She shook her head, trying to whip away the thoughts that this would be a man she wouldn't mind getting to know better. "Just on time. Please, come in. Have a seat at the table and we can discuss more of what you want done."

She held the door open for him as he climbed the three steps into the office part of her trailer. Have mercy, but the man was a tall one. He towered over her five-foot-six-inch frame. He had to be more than six feet of hunk.

"Nice outfit," he said as he looked around.

His gaze scanned the mellow, yellow, vinyl bench seats with the small, pullout table between the seats. On that table sat her coffee machine, some mugs, an open laptop, her calculator and several drawing pads for her designs. The nearby shelves were filled with ink bottles and other tattooing supplies. On the other side of the shelved wall was her work area, which consisted of a tattoo chair, equipment and more shelves with tools of her trade.

"Thanks. It's crowded, but everything I need is here. When I'm out on the road, sometimes tattoo supply stores can be far and few between, so I keep a big stock."

She followed him to the table, assessing his firm-looking ass hugged by a pair of tight, stone-washed blue jeans. He wore an ultra-tight, black t-shirt that illuminated some exceptionally thick pecs.

"You have a tentacle fetish," he stated as he studied the numerous drawings of octopi, squid and all things tentacle she'd drawn, framed and hung on the walls.

Her cheeks grew warm. She sensed in the way his eyes gleamed while he studied each piece that he truly appreciated her art. Finally, a man she just might be interested in.

"I enjoy drawing them."

"That's why you were intrigued by what I sent?" His gaze swept away from her pictures and latched onto her. At the sight of his intense, green eyes, her heart hammered insanely against her chest. Such lovely coloring in those eyes. As green as the ocean on a cloudy day. Very attractive.

"Yes," she admitted in a whisper.

"Do you have any tattoos on your body?"

Oh my. Personal question time or what?

"A couple," she lied. Normally she didn't allow her clients to see the numerous tentacle tattoos that practically devoured every inch of her body. So, she only showed the one gorgeous, plump heart with an arrow shooting through it that she had on the back of her right hand, and the black rose on her left wrist, and wore long sleeves and pants during work hours. Sometimes she showed more of her tattoos to her customers, if she was comfortable with them, and this man made her very uncomfortable, but in a sensual way.

"Would you like a cup of coffee? I've put on a fresh pot. It should be ready." A change of subject was appropriate as it was getting way too warm in here. And the heated way she was reacting to him had nothing to do with the warm breeze blowing in through the several windows she'd propped open this morning.

He smiled and nodded. "Black, please."

She ushered him to the bench seat and quickly grabbed a couple of clean mugs she'd placed on the table earlier. She poured some steaming hot coffee for both of them.

"Yep, you definitely have a tentacle fetish," he grinned.

She jolted at that smile again. This time he showed her an even set of white teeth. Teeth she wouldn't mind exploring with her tongue.

Oh Cat! Stop thinking like this!

He nodded to his coffee mug which had a decal of an octopus with, of course, tons of suction-cupped tentacles on it.

"Caught red-handed," she laughed as she sat down on the bench seat opposite him. From the nearby file folder, she removed the graphic he'd sent.

"I can do this for you, but I wanted to meet you in person because, first of all, so I can discuss with you how the bamboo tattooing procedure I mentioned to you via email will work, that is...if you decide to go ahead with the project and—"

He held up his hand. "No reason to explain. I've done my research. In laymen's terms the bamboo technique gives a more vibrant color. It's less invasive to the flesh and the healing time between sessions is quicker. That's good enough for me. Just tell me how much and I'm all yours."

She'd already figured out how much this would cost him with the ink colors and everything she needed, plus her time, which she'd dropped the price drastically on to entice him into allowing her to do the project. She pulled the estimate from her file folder and placed it in front of him.

Thankfully, the price didn't appear to shock him. He didn't so much as flinch. Yes, he'd definitely done his homework.

"I would have thought it would be way much more." He didn't wait for her answer. "Can we get started right away?

Oh my, but he was in a hurry, wasn't he?

"If you're comfortable with starting now, then yes. I have a few hours open for you today." She'd cleared her schedule and her clients in the hopes he would be as eager as she was to get started. She'd begin slowly, just to break him in easily, since he'd informed her in his email, he'd never had a tattoo before.

"You can undress in the bathroom at the end of the hall. Remove your clothing from your waist down. You'll find paper drapes in there on a shelf. Just wrap one around your waist. Take off your shoes, but you can leave on your socks. You can come back to the tattoo room which is just in the next room here. Last door to your right when you come out of the bathroom." She pointed to the hallway.

"Can't wait," he said. He got up and towered over her. Her gaze dropped to where he'd already started unbuckling his jeans and she didn't miss the impressive bulge between his thighs. Her breath halted in her lungs as he strolled down the narrow hallway of her RV.

Wow! His wide shoulders almost touched the walls. Oh yes, yummy, big man. When the door to the bathroom clicked closed behind him, she hurried to the tattoo room to gather the items she needed.

CALDER CROFT'S THREE hearts crashed against his chest as he undressed in the small bathroom. Being in his human form was hard enough, but how his body was reacting to the beautiful Catalina with the tentacle fetish was just plain annoying, yet very interesting too. He stood in front of the full-length mirror hanging on the inside of the bathroom door and admired his human form. Well, he admired the area below his waist, because the rest of him remained clothed.

His cock appeared quite long, thick and swollen and very erect. Research showed some human women preferred long and thick. He hoped Catalina did too. He'd sensed her attention to him the instant she'd opened the door. Her sexy scent had just about dropped him, and it had taken his every strength to remain standing there as if he wasn't so affected by her nearness. Yes, she was definitely his mate, and he hoped his human shape would do perfectly to seduce her.

It became obvious to him immediately she had no knowledge she was a shifter. He'd seen it in the confused way she had stared at him. He'd noticed her sharp intake of breath when she'd first opened the door. Then erotic interest gleamed in her eyes as she'd sensually inspected him from head to toe. Her entire body had tensed with awareness and her female scent had increased tenfold, informing him she was extremely curious about him.

He assumed her parents hadn't broken the news to her that she might eventually become a shifter. Some waited until their offspring were about to shift before telling them of their heritage. While other parents remained silent about their own abilities, hoping their child would never become a shifter, therefore giving them a somewhat stable environment until the need to tell them ever arose. It looked like the latter had happened with Catalina. He would have to do some quick investigating about her and find out her personal circumstances.

Females took longer to shift than males and he sensed by the intoxicating scent only male Octoposeidons could smell she would be ready to shift soon. He needed to find a way to tell her the truth, to prepare her. She actually thought she was a human, so telling her needed to be handled delicately, gently.

Reaching down, he touched his rigid cock, his warm fingers rubbing the length of the swollen shaft until it was flushed a very nice shade of purplish-blue. He clenched his teeth as the urge to fuck her almost overwhelmed him. He'd been without a female human for a very long time, and it was hard, to say the least, to be around one now, especially a shifter. His best course would be to wait until she turned and take her in the ocean. In Octoposeidon form, females were instinctual. Theirs would be natural mating. In human form, she would be much harder to take. Humans weren't instinctual. Especially the females. Over the centuries, they'd learned to suppress their instincts. They were emotional beings and, in many instances, cautious with the opposite sex.

When he'd first turned, he'd experimented quite a bit, sexually, in his human form. He sensed he would be able to perform and give her the utmost sexual satisfaction. But first he needed to present himself to her, and then he'd let her guide the way.

Blowing out a tense breath, Calder grabbed one of the paper drapes she'd mentioned from a nearby shelf, wrapped it around his waist and let himself out of the bathroom.

Chapter Two

Catalina had all the items she needed set out on her nearby trays when the bathroom door opened and Calder's steps approached down the hall. Odd that she loved the slap of his bare feet against the floor. As he entered her tattoo parlor, everything about her just seemed to zoom in on everything about him. She'd never experienced such an interesting, intense reaction to a man before. But her work ethics were ingrained deeply inside of her, and she would not allow herself to sleep with a client. No matter how much she was attracted to him. And she was definitely attracted to this hunk.

This swish of the paper drape made her turn around. He stood in the doorway, his eyes quite fierce as he stared at her. Oh, if his eyes could fuck, he'd be taking her right here and right now.

She blinked that insane thought away. The man was her client, and she had to keep her mind on her job!

"Please, have a seat and we can get started," she said.

He did as she asked and sat on the chair, placing his socked feet onto the plastic-covered foot stirrups. She slipped on some latex gloves, grabbed the stirrups and moved them outward until she was able to roll her chair in between his wide-spread legs.

"So, I was thinking we should start with measuring the main tentacle...ummm if...you don't mind." Gosh, had she called his cock a tentacle?

Oh my, it truly was getting hot in here. She should turn on the air con. A huge bulge pressed against the paper, leaving her the distinct impression he was aroused. Okay forget the air-con for now. The man was definitely excited. Just as much as she was. What wasn't there to be excited about? She was a woman and she'd be handling his shaft. Totally understandable he might get aroused at that idea.

"How long have you been doing this?" His strong voice sounded confident, as if he allowed himself to have his cock tattooed every day.

"Since I was sixteen, actually," she said as she lifted the paper sheet to reveal his big erection.

Oh boy.

She swore her mouth dropped open at the size of his engorged cock. Have mercy, but the man was built like a stallion. Her pussy pulsed and creamed warmly as visions of him making love to her rolled around in her mind. *Small talk. Yeah, small talk.* She needed to keep him occupied so he wouldn't be frightened off over the way she was staring at him...down there.

Boy, he was big. Too hot in here. Way too hot.

"How did you get interested in tattooing at such an early age?" he asked as she tucked the sheet in and around his erect cock and big balls.

Gosh, she couldn't even think let alone answer his question or begin to measure his shaft to figure out where she should start on him. All she wanted to do was take his swollen erection into her hands and run her fingers along his silky-looking flesh or, better yet, take him into her mouth. Oh yeah. She'd like that too. Very much.

She struggled to gather her thoughts as she tried to figure out which area was best to start on.

"A good friend of mine's older brother had a tattoo shop." Catalina finally managed to pull her thoughts back to her job and return to a semi-professional frame of mind. It wasn't easy, but she began measuring. Sweet heavens, he had a web of veins. Wide girth. Plenty of flesh to work on.

"We went over to his shop a lot because I had a crush on him, so of course I found every excuse under the sun to see him." She laughed, remembering getting her first tattoo by Chad, right smack in the valley of her breasts.

Gosh, she'd loved the way his gaze had languished on her flesh. But Chad had always been strictly professional, much to her disappointment.

"If you had a crush on a tattoo artist then you definitely have tattoos on your body."

She swallowed, loving the way he was looking at her, awaiting her answer with such interest.

"I've got a few," she confessed.

"Don't most people get tattoos so others can see them?" he asked.

She nodded, wrote down the measurements she'd gotten so far. Length, ten inches. Girth, three inches at the base and two and a half inches at the cock head.

Oh boy, his cock looked so damned perfect.

"My tattoos were put in areas were a girl with a crush on a guy would want only him to see."

He grinned at her. "I see."

His smile literally swept her breath away and for a few seconds she was floating wonderfully, like on some cloud, before free-falling back to reality. Reluctantly, she covered his gorgeous erection.

"Okay, now we need to disinfect the area I'll be working on. I received the email with your answers to my questions regarding any allergies and sensitivities, so we're good there."

He nodded.

She cleared her throat, pushed her feet against the ground, letting her stool roll her out from between his legs. She grabbed the nearby tray containing the spray cleanser and disinfectant wipes and swung it toward her client so it would be within easy reach. Then she pulled her chair in between his legs again and noticed he had powerful-looking muscles in his calves.

"Do you work out?" she asked, struggling into small-talk mode again as she slipped off the gloves and put on a fresh pair. In her business, she needed to prevent cross contamination and to be as clean as possible, so with every new step she got rid of the old gloves and put on a new pair.

Once again, she moved his paper sheet to reveal that delightfully engorged cock.

"I run. Jogging along the beach every morning."

Excitement splashed through her. "Me too. I love the way the wind blows against me when I run. And I love the highs that come with running too."

He chuckled. "Those highs are addictive."

She refocused on her job. "Just so you know, this is going to be a bit cold."

"Cold might be what I need," he said in a guttural voice.

Her body hummed and, from the intense way he looked at her with those fuck-me eyes, he desired her.

She kept silent and sprayed cleanser along his hard, swollen erection. He winced at every shot.

"Okay?" she asked.

He cleared his throat and then chuckled. "What do you think?"

She shrugged. "I can't comment. I'm not a guy."

He laughed so deeply, the rich sound seared right into her heart.

"Now for the baby wipes, to make sure every area is reached to prevent infection," she said, her voice low and sexy.

She hoped he didn't read too much into the trembling of her hands as she wrapped her hand around the base of his cock and held tight while she continued to wipe along his erection. Gosh, his flesh was ultra hot and so velvety hard against her palm and fingers. How would he feel sliding into her pussy? How hard would his thrusts be?

Just thinking about having sex with him had her catching a moan. His breath was coming quickly too, and she wondered if he was enjoying the way she held him. What would he do if she suddenly started trailing her fingers up and down? If she leaned over and gobbled that delicious-looking cock head into her mouth and just sucked on him like a lollipop?

Oh my, she was thinking very unprofessionally. She finished wiping around his balls and pulled away. Her breath shook as he blinked. He smiled confidently, seemingly not the least bit embarrassed. So why should she be?

The man was well hung and there was nothing to be embarrassed about. For either of them.

"When I come back, I'll shave you along the area I'll be working on, and then I'll give it another disinfecting before I begin. As I explained in the email, shaving before I do the tattoo will help prevent infection, and I also need to remind you when the time comes to tattoo your other areas, we'll need to shave there to help prevent infection too."

"I understand." Excitement danced in his eyes at that prospect and her heart fluttered. Gosh, he looked so cute when he studied her with his sultry gaze. His eyes shone and the sides of his lips turned upward.

Professional, Cat. Remain professional.

"Okay, next, I'll do some quick calculations and then we'll start outlining the design onto your...um...tentacle."

He laughed, a rich rumble that swept through her like a rushing wave.

"Tentacle fetish, a girl after my own heart."

Oh? What did he mean by that? She chose not to ask. Maybe she would ask later.

She left the room and, with her heart crashing insanely against her chest, she made the calculations at the table where she'd sat earlier with him, figuring out where the suction cups would go. A few minutes later, she had a mind's-eye picture of where everything was going to be placed.

"Okay," she said as she returned to her client. "Um, because of your size, I can get in a few more suction cups." Gosh was her face as red as it felt?

"That's great. The more cups, the better the cling. My girlfriend is going to love it."

Girlfriend? Her excitement shattered. Why did he have to mention he had a girlfriend?

For a moment, she'd been happily fantasizing she'd be able to have his cock tentacle thrusting into her.

"Why the sudden frown? Did I say something wrong?" he asked. His eyes glowed with what she perceived as teasing. But why would he be teasing her? Why try to make her jealous?

Cat shoved away those insane thoughts.

"I'm just hoping your girlfriend will like what you have planned for her," she lied, quickly covering her momentary surprise. She grabbed her outlining pen and placed it on the nearby tray with the measurements plus the drawing he'd sent via email. "I mean some women don't like their men to be covered in tattoos."

She inhaled softly and her pussy clenched when she moved the sheet and revealed that gorgeous cock again.

Intense heat suffused her body at the sight, and she wished she could just dive into the ocean...and cool down.

"*Don't you mean have sex with him in the ocean?*" a naughty little voice whispered.

Yeah, she'd like that. Sex with this stranger. His tentacle plunging into her. No strings. Nice.

"She'll love this," he said with such confidence she suddenly had no doubt his girlfriend would like it.

"Um, did you want your foreskin tattooed also?" she asked, hoping he'd say yes. She caught her breath as his gaze darkened with arousal. *Getting way too hot*!

"I mean... It'll be quite delicate. Uncomfortable when I do it. But the discomfort will only last a few hours."

"Which way will look better?"

Oh boy. Cheeks flaming. Body trembling. Pussy creaming.

"With the foreskin included," she admitted, wishing she could slap a bunch of ice cubes over her burning cheeks.

He grinned and her pussy did some mighty sensual flip-flops and warm creaming.

Gazing at his engorged cock, she tried to keep a steady hand as she reached for the can of shaving cream she'd placed on another nearby tray. She began to spray the lather onto him.

He sucked in a sharp breath, and she stopped.

"Sorry, should have warned you."

"It's not that." He peered at her with an extreme concentration, one that said he rather enjoyed her spraying lather onto his shaft.

Her cheeks were on fire now.

"Oh," she whispered, understanding, and tried really hard to focus back on her job.

After a moment of silence, he asked, "Do you have a boyfriend? Or are you married?"

"No. I'm a loner. Prefer to stay that way," she said as she continued spraying.

He didn't say anything, which was good.

When she had his entire cock lathered, she uncapped the plastic from the disposable razor and held the tip of his erection. Ignoring another rush of his breath, she began to shave him carefully.

Beneath her fingertips, his flesh vibrated ever so slightly. He obviously enjoyed her touches. His cock pulsed and the heat from his member seared her fingers. She hurried the task, gliding up and down until she'd shaved its entirety. He could have shaved himself, but she'd wanted to make sure it was done right.

Yeah, right. More like you wanted to get another good look at him. Touch him some more.

"Okay here comes more. I'll just do a little around near the base area," she warned him as she lifted his shaft, grabbed the shaving cream and sprayed his scrotum.

"Shit," he whispered.

"Sorry."

"Don't be."

She tried not to read into what he'd just said, but what else could she do? His eyes were scrunched tight as she proceeded to shave along where the base of his erection and scrotum met. Quick glances at his face revealed muscles twitching in his strong jawline. It seemed as if he was holding onto a thread of self-control.

Wow. He certainly was a virile man, wasn't he?

She completed the shaving then wiped the area clean before spraying on another dose of disinfectant.

"There, all done. Now the fun part starts."

His breath continued heavily and when he popped open his eyes, they sparkled, and his eyelids appeared drowsy with arousal.

She responded at the intense way he gazed at her. Heat suffused her entire body, and her breath came soft and sultry. She swallowed and quickly grabbed her tracing pen. "I'll start at the base and work toward the tip."

"You're the boss." His voice was thick and sensual, stroking her senses.

Yeah, well, if she were the boss, she'd be straddling him about now. She held her breath as she outlined the area she'd work on today.

"I plan on doing this in small patches. Every day a patch until we're finished. After I'm done with today's session, we can check the appointment book and schedule you in."

"Great. So, how do you work? Do you need quiet to tattoo or lots of noise?" he asked.

"Depends on how hard the tattoo is. If it's easy, I can talk. If it's hard," *like your cock*, "I need to concentrate."

"Right now, it's hard," she admitted, avoiding his gaze. *Oh yeah, baby, you are so hard.*

She swallowed and eased a soft breath into her lungs. He smelled way too good too. Kind of like when she stood on a beach on a sunny day—everything fresh and sparking clean with a delicate hint of salt in the breeze. That's exactly how he smelled. Like he belonged near the ocean or something. For a split second, she imagined she really was standing on a pristine beach with the warm sand sifting past her bare toes. Naked, after having come out of the water. He would be there with her. Sparkles of water dripping off his heavily muscled body.

She blinked and the awesome vision disintegrated. Oh man, for a bit she'd felt as if she'd been right *there* on the beach. Wow! She had it bad for this guy, didn't she?

"It looks fantastic," he said softly.

Huh?

She followed his gaze downward and blinked in utter disbelief as a full outline of a tentacle, complete with suckers, ran up his cock.

What the fuck?

She didn't even remember drawing it.

Okay, this was way too weird. How could she not remember drawing this outline? She hadn't wanted to do the entire penis. Just pieces. But it looked perfect.

"You were really into it, I'm impressed. I can't wait to see how it looks with color and shading," he continued.

The excitement lacing his voice seemed to enter her bloodstream, pushing aside her concern for not remembering. Yeah, she had artistic highs where she got lost in a tattoo, but the customer always ripped her out of it with a cough or something. She bit her lip as she surveyed her work. She had to admit it did look fantastic, even if it was just an outline.

"I'm glad you're happy with it. Give me a few minutes to get the colors together. You should stand up and stretch and walk around."

What in the world had just happened to her? Why didn't she remember drawing that outline?

Ignoring her suddenly trembling hands, she placed her pen on the nearby tray, removed her gloves, tossed them in the wastebasket and rolled her chair away from him.

To her surprise, he didn't even cover his lower half as he stood. His cock was so engorged it curled upward against his belly as he padded past her.

"Coffee? I need coffee. Can I get you a cup?" he asked as he paused in the doorway.

"No, thanks." Like, wasn't she jittery enough?

She sighed with relief as he left the room. His presence had overpowered her, and she could actually think now. She'd started drawing on his flesh and then she'd been on the beach with him. It had seemed so lifelike. So real. *Too* freaking real. Artistic high? Could one happen so quickly during a project? It had never happened so fast before. But it did happen. She could lose hours on a tattoo, and it would seem as if only a few minutes had gone by. Just like now. She gazed at the clock. Half an hour.

Absolutely freaking amazing!

Okay, she needed to get the colors next. Yes, the ink colors. She would need black for the outline, and she would mix some of the other colors she wanted too.

My, oh my, but she was so wonderfully hot! And aware of him. And aroused. It was insane. But in an erotic kind of way. Catalina hurried to grab the ink bottles she needed from a nearby shelf and set up her workstation.

CALDER SLOWLY SIPPED his black coffee and listened for more movement from the tattoo parlor. He could sense Catalina was confused due to the fact she'd gone into a trance while she'd traced the outline on his cock. Her spell was an indication she was going to shapeshift sooner than he'd anticipated. Obviously, she had no clue of her true heritage, but over the next few days she would begin to question the changes in her body and wonder about the blackouts that were common before a first shift.

He blew out a hot breath as his cock hardened even more. He didn't even need to stroke himself into arousal now. Just thinking of her was all he needed.

He sipped more coffee, enjoying the soothing way it melted along his parched throat. He enjoyed being a human mainly because he was addicted to the coffee.

Tonight, before he turned and went into the ocean, he'd make sure he switched on the auto brew, so when he returned from the depths his coffee would be ready and hot for him. Just like Catalina would be hot and ready for him the next time he came here. He could hardly wait.

"OKAY, YOU'RE GOING to feel some pain," Catalina warned. "There will be some sharp pinpricks, but I need you to hold still." After setting up her inks and other supplies, she'd washed her hands again, slipped on a new pair of latex gloves and dashed some numbing gel and healing ointment on the area she would begin tattooing.

"I'm into a bit of pain." He grinned at her and her tummy somersaulted.

Oh man, she wished he wouldn't do that. His smile was lethal to her visual senses. Heck he was lethal to all her senses. Yet, miraculously, her concentration seemed focused and unbelievably clear as she dipped her bamboo tipped with needles into the black ink and moved over to the base of his shaft. She asked him to hold his cock steady, and he wrapped his fingers around his cock head, holding himself still. She didn't dare look up to gaze into his eyes, because she just knew what she'd find there. Arousal, excitement and that exquisite need for sexual release. His and hers.

Blowing out a steadying breath, she slipped the bamboo stalk between her middle finger and forefinger and let it lean against the area between her thumb and forefinger, then began a gentle up and down motion, tapping along the lines on his flesh.

After a few seconds, she stopped and forced herself to cast her gaze at him. "Okay?"

He nodded. "Not bad, I expected worse. Please, do continue. It feels kind of pleasant."

"Wish all my customers said that," she said and began tapping again.

Thankfully, he remained silent as she allowed the bamboo stalk to slide quickly and confidently against his flesh. Tattooing always relaxed her, and it relaxed her now too as she pummeled his hard and swollen erection, following the black lines. His heavy flesh pulsed erotically against her fingers. What would he say if she stopped tattooing and slipped off her shorts and panties and just slid his juicy cock into her vagina as she sat on his lap? Gosh, she hadn't even realized how sexy a man could look with his thighs spread and his feet settled into her stirrups. She swore when he left, she would fantasize about those foot stirrups.

She'd undress in front of him. Kind of like an erotic dancer. She'd take off her clothing seductively, leisurely, starting with her blouse first...

STARING AT HIM WHILE she slowly unbuttoned her shirt, his eyes darkened as if an erotic storm was swirling within him. She removed her blouse and then her bra. Her breasts spilled free for his heated gaze.

She twirled her bra in the air like a lasso before tossing it at him. He caught it with his foot and grinned at her.

"What do I look like? A garment holder?" he whispered, the tip of his pink tongue pushing out from between his lush lips.

She didn't reply, her gaze sweeping to that enticing tongue of his. She unclasped the button on her jeans, slipping down the zipper. He tensed, the muscles in his chest and shoulders jumping magnificently as his hands grabbed the armrest of the tattoo chair. She loved that he was fighting for self-control.

She swallowed as she continued, peeling her jeans over her wide hips. He sucked in a breath as she stepped out of them.

"If you go any further, I can't be responsible for what happens next," he whispered hoarsely.

Oh, she loved the tortured coarseness in his voice. It made her tremble. Made her daring. She'd never felt daring with a man.

Until him.

Stepping closer, between his wide-spread legs, she inhaled and moaned as he reached out and cupped her heavy breasts. His hands were warm as he cradled her.

"Move closer," he whispered.

She whimpered as she leaned in, and he kissed the tight tip of one of her breasts.

Oh, so gentle. So beautiful.

He opened his mouth and sucked her sensitive nipple inside. His mouth was so hot she literally ached there. His teeth nipped delicately, unleashing an incredible pulsing deep inside her vagina. Oh wow, she'd never been this wanton before with a man's mouth on her breast.

He tugged on her nipple and then laved his tongue around the peak. His mouth made love to her, and she couldn't stop her gasps as he moved on to her other breast and continued to work his wonderful magic. She sensed he was pushing her toward something awesome as he tugged gently then bit tenderly.

Her breath came faster and was soon out of control. She arched closer to him, slipping her hands against his waist, holding him tight as his suckling grew firmer, rougher. The incredible tingles racing through her spun into something desperate and unmanageable.

Sharp desire coursed through her, rocked her, and she sailed right along with it. His tongue lashed her like a whip, the sweet bite of his sharp teeth erotic pinpricks. Suddenly her entire body throbbed with intense need, and she exploded on a groan as she quickly rubbed her pussy against his thick shaft. She wanted to reach down and grab his cock and slip his thickness inside her, but his hands were suddenly on her hands, holding them firmly on his waist, keeping her hostage as she pressed and gyrated against his hot erection.

She cried out as her pussy spasmed around empty air, her body climaxing. The deep shudders were endless as she gyrated and moaned and drowned in the vortex. Her mind splintered and her body instinctively enjoyed his gift of pleasure.

Soon, the spasms ebbed away and their heavy breathing burst through the small room. Oh wow! She'd never climaxed while a man fucked her breasts with his mouth.

SHE BLEW OUT A FIERCE breath as sudden reality crashed in around her and she blinked.

The first thing she noticed was her clothing. She hadn't removed them at all! Somehow, she'd slipped into one heck of a naughty fantasy. The second thing she noticed was his awesome tentacle tattoo. Vibrant colors literally leapt off his cock. The greens, the gray and black shadings, the circles of suction cups were so lifelike. His cock seriously looked like a tentacle.

Oh. My. Goodness.

"Your work is breathtaking," he whispered as he stared directly at her with an intensity that snapped like a live wire right into her core.

What the hell had just happened? Why was he acting as if everything was normal? Anxiety burst through her, but she managed to shake it off.

"Um...thanks." Her voice came out strangled and harsh.

Have mercy! Had she gone into some sort of artistic, erotic high? She swore she could not remember tattooing his entire cock. It should have taken her the course of several days to get such an intricate design.

And yet... She glanced at her clock. Four hours had gone by! It seemed like only a few minutes. What in the world was wrong with her?

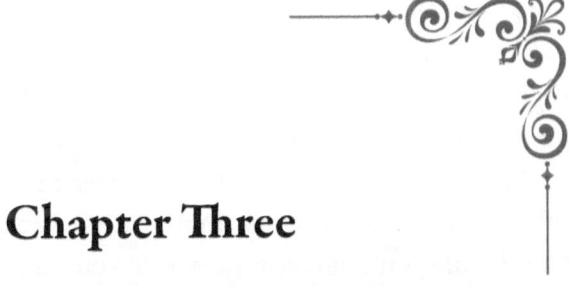

Chapter Three

She was frightened. Fear flashed in her pretty blue eyes as she spread the soothing ointment all over his cock with freshly gloved hands. Her fingers trembled against his hot, aching flesh and her breathing was erratic. She would be questioning what had happened to her. He pondered whether he should tell her that many times, sometimes days and even hours before a female shifted, she went into erotic spells. Part of her mind splintered into hot, sexual fantasies, while another part continued as if nothing was happening. Any human male couldn't even tell, but Calder could. Her sexy enticing scent had increased tenfold the instant she'd slipped into the mind trance, and it had taken every ounce of his strength to remain seated in his chair when all he'd wanted to do was start fucking her.

It had been hell. It was still hell. He just wanted to dive into her fragrance, her mind and body and simply make love to her.

No, he wouldn't tell her. She would have to undergo more changes, and she would have to have more questions before she would be receptive to even considering her true heritage as a possibility. Right now, he sensed she wasn't ready for the truth. Not yet.

He gritted his teeth as her sensual caresses made love to his human flesh. His cock was so engorged and a little sore too but enduring the needles piercing his tender tissue had been worth it.

"This tattoo lube will help prevent infection and promote healing. It has all natural ingredients like vitamin E and aloe vera to help heal."

Her voice was shaky. He hoped she would be all right. He would like to stay and keep her company, to soothe her, but he didn't wish to frighten her any more due to the fact he could barely keep his hands to himself and all he wanted to do was touch her.

"Before you leave, I'll give you more instructions plus your own tube of lube. Because it's a bamboo tattoo, you'll have to wait only one hour before you can take a swim or go out in the sun. It'll be healed in a day."

He nodded. He'd done his homework on bamboo tattooing, and it was different than getting a machine tat.

"Because this technique allows the needles to barely break the skin to get the color and there's minimal damage, you'll be ready to have another one in a day or two. The pain is temporary and as you can see the detailing is very accurate and lifelike."

"You sound surprised," he teased.

She tried to smile, but it came off wobbly. She still hadn't fully recuperated from her mind clicking out. Understandable.

"And it barely hurts."

She smiled, obviously pleased. "Well, at least I'm not using bamboo thorns like the ancient cultures did."

Ouch!

She covered his cock with the paper drape, removed her gloves, tossed them into a wastebasket, and then handed him the bamboo pole she'd used on him, minus the needles, which she'd thrown into a nearby hazard container. "For you. A souvenir. I never use the same bamboo pole twice. It cuts out cross contamination in my workspace."

"Thanks." It would be a very nice souvenir. His first tattoo, one of many he hoped, by his mate. She wheeled her chair away from between his legs then stood. She stretched like a cat, her arms and hands going up into the air, her lush breasts poking against a work apron which covered the front of her blouse and dropped to mid-thigh.

"I'll leave you to get dressed," she said. "Meet me be back out in the main foyer and we'll schedule you in."

She turned and briskly left the room.

Having her out of his sight brought a sadness he'd never experienced before, but the Ancients had said this would be expected. Once she turned, the intensity of their need for each other would only increase. It was the way of their species. One of many built-in procreation instincts that kept mates close to each other, so others of their species had less chance of trying to move in on one's mate.

He shifted his legs from the stirrups. They were quite understandably sore and stiff from lack of movement, and suddenly he craved his tentacles and some leisurely swimming through the fluidity of the water. It was much easier living in the ocean depths. Then all his limbs were loose and limber. He couldn't wait for her to turn so she could join him and experience instinctual mating. But he would have to wait. He sighed with frustration and headed to the bathroom to retrieve his clothing.

"ARE YOU SERIOUS?" CATALINA'S friend Misty gasped for the tenth time as Catalina continued to relay what had happened to her while she'd been tattooing Calder. They'd been lying on their bellies for an hour, upon their air mattresses, on the almost-secluded, white sandy beach behind Cat's RV, soaking up some late-evening sunshine.

"You blanked out?"

Concern marred her friend's features and Catalina regretted having confessed. Misty would only worry. She was like that. She worried about every little thing.

"I think you should see my doctor. Maybe you've got a brain tumor or something."

Oh, for heaven's sake. Yep, she definitely shouldn't have shared what had happened.

"No, I don't have a brain tumor, Misty. It was some kind of artistic high. I'm sure of it," she lied as she tried to ease the anxiety flaring in Misty's eyes.

"Do you really think so?"

No. But Catalina forced herself to smile, reached out and grabbed one of Misty's hands.

"I really think so," she lied again. "Calder didn't seem the least bit suspicious anything had happened. He said I had done a wonderful job. So obviously whatever happened I was able to keep working through it, so it must have been an artistic high." The weirdest and coolest one she'd ever had.

Relief splashed through Misty's face. She had taken the bait. "Now let's figure out exactly how we can get this incredible guy into your bed."

Catalina rolled her eyes. Leave it to Misty to try her matchmaking. "He's not available."

Misty frowned and pounded the sand with her fist. "Shit. The wife. Of course, I should have known some lucky chick would get the well-hung man who is into the same fetish as you."

"Actually—" Cat stopped as Misty's eyes widened with expectation. She should have kept her mouth shut.

"Yeah...go on." Misty squealed, giving her head a curious tilt that made Cat almost laugh out loud at how cute and excited her friend looked.

"Never mind."

"He's unhappily married?" she prodded, her mouth dropping open with anticipation.

"Let's just get off the topic. I want to have some fun. Let's go swimming." Suddenly Cat had this really intense need to take a dip in the ocean.

She turned over and rolled off her mattress onto the sandy beach. Standing, she frowned when Misty didn't follow. Her friend remained on her tummy; arms tucked beneath her chin. But from this angle, Cat could tell Misty was smiling quite happily. Matchmaking thoughts again. That was okay, though. The urge to head into the ocean was growing stronger and she just wanted to be alone with it.

"Okay, so he's not married," Cat confessed. "But he's got a girlfriend with a tentacle fetish and that's why he's giving her a tattoo. It's a present to her."

Misty gazed up at her. "And you've got the same fetish. The man is available, girlfriend. A-v-a-i-l-a-b-l-e. No wedding ring means he is still available."

Disappointment rocked Cat. She'd never go after a man who was so obviously in love with another woman. So, in love he was getting her something as permanent as a tattoo.

"I don't steal boyfriends, Misty. You know me better than that."

Misty grimaced and closed her eyes and settled her head back onto her arms, as if she was about to take a nap, which she usually did when she came over to visit and they lay on the beach.

"Yeah, I know," Misty said sadly. "And with that kind of attitude you're never going to catch a man, Cat."

Well, then if that's the way it had to be, then so be it. Cat grabbed her mattress, shoving it under her right arm before padding barefoot toward the gently lapping ocean.

The sun was just setting, and it sat like a giant ball right on top of the ocean, casting orange sparkles across the small waves. As her toes dipped into the cool water, all the tension from today's happenings suddenly seemed to melt out of her body and slip into the water.

Despite the conversation she'd just had with Misty about not going after another woman's man, she couldn't stop thinking about Calder. Couldn't wait to see him again. She'd set up their next appointment for the day after tomorrow because she had already been booked solid for the following day. She'd blocked out the entire afternoon for him.

He would have a day of healing and, when he came back, she'd be able to go on to tattoo the octopus across his belly and abdomen. If she didn't zone out like she'd done today, and didn't slip into another odd, artistic high, she could do the outline of the octopus in that time frame. Then start on coloring and some shadowing, leaving the other tentacles he wanted for other days. She'd leave the rose-enshrouding heart with the keyhole for last.

She gazed down at herself as she slipped up to her knees in the water. She'd had a friend tattoo artist do an octopus on her lower back, with tentacles wrapping around her waist and one going down the back of each of her legs. She had a couple of tentacles stretching up her belly toward her breasts too. The ones on her front she'd tattooed herself. She'd spent many hours on them. They were so lifelike. Just as beautiful as the tentacle she'd drawn on Calder's cock. She'd used many of the same colors. Various shades of greens, grays and blacks, with white-capped waves splashing all around the long, swollen tentacles.

She still didn't understand how she'd been able to tattoo Calder without even remembering doing it, especially since she'd been looking so forward to this project. This zoning-out thing was really strange, and it was weird too that she wasn't more panicked.

Cat walked farther into the ocean, the water now embracing her breasts. She let the air mattress float on the water beside her and held it with one hand, readying it so she could shove her upper body on top and kick her way farther out.

But instead of following through on her intention, she smiled as she continued to look down. Beneath the water's edge, her tattoos seemed to come alive, moving back and forth on her body like arms beckoning her to dive under and swim like the animals. To be free and just float through the water, light and weightless. Her arms and legs transformed into tentacles, stroking the cool liquid with ease. She imagined herself as a squid or an octopus or some sea creature, her tentacles waving at her mate.

Oh yes, she would definitely have a sexual partner. Catalina smiled and incredible warmth burst inside her as she imagined having a male companion to swim with, to make love with and to love.

A tentacle of her partner would magically strip off her bikini top and bottom and wrap around each of her breasts, the suction cups holding her tightly, while two other tentacles would stroke her nipples until they were tight and achy. A swollen, hot appendage would snugly encircle her waist, holding her steady while yet another slipped into her ass.

She gasped at the sensual fullness as he explored her. The tip of another tentacle rubbed against her sensitive clit, massaging until her breath came faster and carnal urges shivered through her core. She moaned as another tentacle slid into her vagina, the warm, velvety flesh sliding deep, the suction cups snapping against long-dormant nerve endings.

She sucked in a sharp breath as both tentacles eased from her vagina and ass then plunged back in. Another thrust erotically into her mouth. The thought she was being triple penetrated rushed her mind.

Very ingenious to triple penetrate. After the initial shock of what he had done, she reached out her own tentacles which had only moments ago been her arms and legs.

Awesome to be able to shift like this. But it was just a dream. A wicked fantasy. And she was going with it.

Wrapping one of her tentacles around the base of his engorged cock, a cock that looked just like Calder's newly tattooed shaft, she held him tightly, using another tentacle to erotically caress his cock head. It was really cool, this fantasy.

Aside from her arms and legs, the rest of her was the same as she floated beneath the water. Calder drifted in front of her, his arms and legs had turned into long, swollen tentacles too, yet the rest of him remained human. His head, muscular chest, his torso, his tattooed cock, all looked the same.

His eyes were closed as he held on to her. His thrusts continued, growing harder and more desperate. His tentacles swelled, pulsing, getting hotter inside of her. She firmly held his cock while she continued stroking his flesh.

They made love, thrashing in the water. Air bubbles surrounded them and hid them from prying fish, eager to watch. Pleasure rocked her as he kept up the triple penetrations. Spasms raced through her breasts, her vagina, her ass. They pummeled her, gripped her and loved her.

She gasped in the water, her body trembling into the orgasm, and vaguely realized she could breathe the liquid. But that discovery was quickly forgotten as a hot limb pressed into her mouth. He continued thrusting his tentacles into her, and then she was flying into another climax.

She exploded. Her mind splintered, her body shuddered, and his tentacles pulsed and tightened as he tensed and trembled right along with her. They floated that way through the bubbles, their tentacles holding and caressing each other. Intuition told her he was satisfied and loving the after-sex ambiance. It was as if she was in tune with his body, his instincts, his love for her. As if they were one being.

He opened his eyes and suddenly everything seemed real. Too real.

Gorgeous, green eyes blinked at her and shock crashed through Catalina like a rogue, ocean wave. She *really* was underwater. Breathing. What the heck?

What had just happened wasn't a fantasy. It was real! The shock suddenly made it difficult to breathe and terror ripped through her as she thought about drowning down here. Then, without warning, she was thrust away from him and upward. Ripped from his embrace, pummeling up through the murky liquid like a rocket. Her head broke free from the water and she frantically gasped for air.

"Cat! Cat! Oh my God! There she is! There she is!" Misty's panicked shrieks echoed in Cat's ears from somewhere behind her.

Cat's feet miraculously touched the sandy ocean ground, and she stood neck deep in the water. Stunned at what had just happened, she couldn't understand how she suddenly had feet and arms again. Heck, she couldn't get a grip on how she could have so easily accepted she'd just had tentacles, and that Calder had been part-human, part-tentacle man and had been making love to her.

Confusion gripped her and she turned around and gasped as a bright light shone over the half-foot waves, blinding her.

What happened? Why was she in the water? Where was her air mattress?

"Miss. Miss. Are you alright?" Some guy called to her as he furiously paddled a surfboard through the surrounding darkness. An irritating light arrowed at her from the newcomer and suddenly all she wanted to do was dive back under the water. Back into the love and pleasure of being with Calder.

Catalina shook her head. No, she must be going crazy. Not Calder. But something had tugged her under the water. Something delightful.

A shark? An octopus? She remembered tentacles. Lots of them wrapped around her, pulsing in and out of her. She moaned softly, reliving the powerful thrusts and magnificent orgasms. But, she hadn't been human...

She'd been one of whatever the hell she'd been. She'd had tentacles herself.

"Cat? Is she all right?" Misty's voice shrieked through her confusion. How in the world had Misty seen her? It was so dark on the beach Cat couldn't even see the shoreline.

"Miss, your friend is really worried. Can you talk to me?" The man was right beside her now, belly down on his surfboard, a dark silhouette on the water's surface. That irritating light was slicing into her eyes again.

She held up her hand to shield the light. "I'm fine. I just went out too far."

"I don't know. You were gone pretty long. We were all looking. We couldn't see you. I'm going to take you to the first-aid station and get you checked out."

He slipped off his surfboard and into the water beside her. He wore a helmet, and the light came off the front of it.

Her rescuer was just a young guy of maybe eighteen years.

"I'm going to hoist you up on my board and then climb on top and paddle behind you. Are you okay with that?"

She nodded numbly, but then suddenly stopped. Her bikini top was missing!

"Um, no. No. I'm fine. I'll walk back."

"That's a bad idea, miss. You might slip under again."

Again? Yes, yes, she had been under the water. But how had she been able to breathe? How in the world was she going to explain her missing top? She ran her fingers lower and froze when she touched cool skin. Her bikini bottoms were gone too! She was completely naked.

Oh goodness. Something had definitely happened in the water. She began to tremble.

"I'll just hang on to the surfboard and walk with you," she compromised.

"Okay, but that's against my better judgment." He hoisted his lean form back onto the board.

She only took a few steps before the water came to just above the curves of her breasts. She stopped and finally confessed her situation. Or at least what she hoped he would believe to be her situation.

"I...actually I don't want to scare my friend. I got caught in an undertow. My top got ripped off and I'm really cold. Can you just go back to her and get my throw?"

"I'll get your friend to bring it out."

"No, please. I'd rather you go and get it. I need a moment to compose myself." Actually, she needed a few moments to reorient herself and try to figure out what had happened.

The man nodded. "Sure. Sure. But once again. This is against my better judgment." He slipped off his board again. "Here, hold on to this. Tight. I'll get it."

"Thanks."

When he left, she couldn't help but look back out across the ocean in the direction she instinctively knew she'd been. The sun had set. The sky had turned a velvety, dark purple, bursting with glistening, white stars. Nothing moved on the quiet surface of the ocean. Not a wave. Not even a ripple.

Her breath backed up at the beautiful glass-like surface of the endless ocean. Far in the distance, a roll of white puffy clouds danced on the horizon and a large white houseboat was anchored out there too.

As she stared at it, her shattered nerves seemed to calm, just like she'd calmed earlier when she'd first gone into the water. A beautiful rainbow slowly arched over the boat. Then all too quickly the rainbow disappeared, and the boat was swallowed up by darkness.

She should be relieved that she'd somehow gotten free of whatever had held her. Instead, she yearned to go back out there. To be with him.

With Calder?

Oh yeah, she must be losing her mind. Big-time.

CALDER'S THREE HEARTS pounded madly as he swam near his houseboat, his body satiated from the quick, intense sex he'd just had with Catalina. He hadn't anticipated taking her tonight. He'd anchored his houseboat about a mile off the beach from where her RV campsite was located and watched the area with binoculars, hoping to catch a glimpse of her. When, in the late afternoon, Catalina and another woman around Cat's age came out to lie on the beach, his hearts had soared. He'd waited on his houseboat, loving the way those tentacle tattoos hugged the backs of her legs and wrapped around her waist. Damn, she was sexy. He kind of felt guilty spying on her, but after leaving her today, he'd only wanted to see her again.

While he thought about her, Calder slowly crawled with his tentacles. He'd been so intent on watching Cat, he'd almost shifted on the houseboat. Usually, he found a more secluded spot to anchor for the night, but tonight he'd barely hit the water before he began turning. It had been a close call, but well worth hanging around the area.

He'd loved curling his tentacles around her breasts, tweaking her nipples. Watching how her pretty mouth parted and panted. She hadn't even realized she'd turned. It was normal in the beginning not to realize what was happening. But her brain would catch up.

He could still feel her cool silky flesh tingling against his suction cups where he'd latched onto her newly formed limbs. Throbbing arousal pulsed through his tentacles, especially the ones that had penetrated her.

He hadn't realized she'd shifted until her sexy scent embraced him in the water. His instincts to mate with her had kicked in and, using his tentacles, he swam quickly and found her.

She'd been languishing on the surface of the ocean. The fact her head was underwater, and she'd been breathing made him realize the gills, prevalent to their species, had formed behind her ears. He'd aligned with her and brought her down to the ocean floor and, following his instincts, he'd made love to her.

After the sex, he'd sensed she was changing back to human form, and he'd propelled her to the top of the water. The sudden shift in Octoposeidons wasn't uncommon in the first few days when a female or male entered the beginning of their change. Some, when in their human form, drowned due to the unexpected shift back and forth, unless of course they had an experienced one around to help them. The same could be said when shifting from human to Octoposeidon on land, except this was called dry drowning.

He focused his thoughts back on Catalina.

She was probably frightened. Didn't know what had happened. Perhaps she was even thinking she was going insane. He should go to her and explain. He shouldn't have waited today. He should have warned her what would be happening to her arms and legs and that she would be able to breathe beneath the water during the nights. He doubted she would have believed him anyway. But now that the mating had begun, she would experience unexplained sexual urges.

A new sense of desperation swept through him. He wished he could be there to comfort her and reassure her she wasn't losing her mind. But he wouldn't be able to shift again until the first rays of sunlight sparkled against the ocean water. Until then, he was trapped here beneath the ocean. Without her.

In the near distance, he spied Catalina's bikini top and bottom floating close to each other about a foot below the surface and his hearts quickened with excitement. Propelling himself through the current, he grabbed each piece. Using the sensory organs on his tentacles he took in her scent and within a second it turned his body into an agonizing ball of alertness. Her female scent was all over the material. He absolutely loved her sexy smell. Like wildflowers and ocean waves and female.

Calder closed his eyes and curled his tentacles tighter around the suit pieces, embracing them, wishing she was here. For the first time in his entire shapeshifting life, he couldn't wait until morning. Couldn't wait until he had land legs again. Couldn't wait to be with Catalina.

CATALINA TREMBLED FROM head to toe as she stepped into her tiny shower. Despite her earlier comfort at seeing that wonderful rainbow out on the ocean, over that houseboat, her relief had collapsed as Misty ran down the beach and into the water to hug her with such fierceness it unnerved Cat. There were several other people milling around, concerned for her safety, and all she wanted to do was get to the privacy of her RV.

"My God! I thought you were dead. I was sleeping for a good hour. One second you were there and then I drifted off to sleep, and when I woke up, I couldn't find you. Someone said they saw a red air mattress about a mile out in the ocean and then I really freaked. And like I told the lifeguard, you would have woken me up if you'd decided to go somewhere. I was about to call 9-1-1."

"She should go to the first-aid shack so I can check her out," the young man said.

"I'm fine. Seriously," she lied. "I'd just like to get back to my RV and get changed."

Thankfully her throw covered all necessary private parts and, because she'd remained in the deep water and put the throw on while there, it was sopping wet, and she was truly cold.

"I should have asked you these questions earlier, but you mentioned an undertow. Did you black out? Hit your head? Anything like that?" the lifeguard questioned. He shifted nervously and Cat figured maybe he hadn't followed proper protocol about calling 9-1-1 due to his inexperience or panic.

"Oh my God, Cat! You could have drowned," Misty cried and once again threw her arms around Catalina.

"I'm fine. Believe me. I just got pulled out and had to swim back."

The lifeguard didn't appear to believe her as he frowned and shook his head. Gosh was she that transparent?

Thankfully, he went to report the incident, but Misty had been like a clinging vine as she'd brought Cat to her RV and insisted on spending the night. But Cat had been adamant Misty was overreacting, reminding her friend she would be late for her date with a hottie fireman on her one night off. It had been hell getting her to leave, but Cat had just wanted to be alone to think.

Thank God for dates.

Catalina stepped into the shower and the warm water beat down against her pleasantly sore nipples. Gosh, not only were her nipples tender, but the harsh crash of water made them bead and harden with exquisite arousal. Actually, the silky water splashing against her skin made her flesh tingle wonderfully, as if the liquid were embracing her, hugging her, comforting her. It was weird to think about water being her friend, especially after what had happened out in the ocean.

She shivered as she remembered looking down at herself, admiring her tentacle tattoos and imagining them coming to life.

Maybe she *had* been caught in an undertow and conked her head. Maybe she had imagined her arms and legs being tentacles and mating with some half-human, tentacle man who looked like Calder. Yeah, she must have hit her head, and maybe it had been some Dorothy-in-the-Land-of-Oz adventure?

She sighed heavily and reached for her peach-scented soap. Whatever had happened, she'd blacked out today. Twice. All this blacking out was just not normal. But both times she'd fantasized about Calder. *Huh, odd.* Maybe Misty was right. Maybe she should go see a doctor.

Lathering her body, she paid particular attention to her sensitive pussy and sore ass. Triple penetrated? By tentacles? Those were crazy ideas. Really crazy. If she went to a doctor and explained what she believed had happened, she'd be thrown into a mental institution for observation or, at the very least, told to have brain tests done. Tests she just didn't have the money for since she wasn't even insured!

No, she would just have to take a wait-and-see approach.

After shampooing her hair and rinsing her soap, she turned off the faucets, slid open her glass shower door and stepped into her bathroom. Just then, she noticed a folded piece of paper lying on the floor.

Picking it up, she unfolded it and found a credit card inside. The paper was a receipt made out to Calder for a boat slip rental. The credit card was in his name.

Oh dear. It must have slipped out of his pants when he'd hung them up. He might need the card tomorrow. The poor guy was probably frantically looking for it.

The receipt was dated yesterday and the marina where he supposedly was renting a slip was only about a half an hour walk up the beach.

Huh. She should phone him, let him know she had his card.

Wrapping a towel around her body, she treaded barefoot to the main foyer of her RV. Sitting at her bench seat, she quickly went through her files on her laptop and found the phone number he'd given her. Her heart picked up speed and she dialed his number. She wasn't sure if she was relieved or disappointed the call went straight to voice mail. She shivered at the intoxicating sound of his deep voice. Strong and confident. Listening to him soothed her rattled nerves and, at the beep, she left a message and hung up.

Placing the card and receipt in a nearby cupboard, she strolled back into her tattoo room, checked on the sterilization equipment and made sure everything else was okay. She stared at the footrests where Calder had placed his feet earlier today.

It was while she'd been tattooing him the first blackout had occurred. Actually, she'd fantasized about him while tattooing. Yet the tattoo hadn't suffered due to her fantasizing, and when she'd come out of whatever spell she'd been in, he hadn't seemed to notice. So, what did she have, a split personality?

Yeah right. Suddenly she could breathe under water like the ocean creatures. As if maybe her tentacle fetish had manifested into something...fantastical? Gosh! Was that even a word? A fantasy world to escape reality? Too much stress? Or had she pricked her finger and gotten some ink into her veins and hallucinated. She'd seen a movie about that once.

The shrill ring of her cell phone, echoing from the bathroom, made her scream as a jolt of surprise shot through her. She quickly padded down the hallway to get it.

Gosh! Was she ever jumpy. She needed to chill because she normally wasn't the nervous type. But who could blame her? Especially after today's strange events.

She noticed Misty's number on her caller display and answered, knowing her friend was checking up on her, but it warmed her heart to know Misty really cared.

"Hey, how's the date going?" Cat asked quickly, hoping to deflect Misty's worry.

"Quit trying to change the subject. How are you?"

Great.

"I told you before you left that I was fine."

"I just want to make sure. You know me. Do you have a headache or dizziness or anything like that? Chuck wants to know."

Cat grinned. Yeah, Misty's worrying irritated her sometimes, but not right now.

"Chuck. The fireman boyfriend who is going to make you so hot tonight?" Cat teased.

Misty didn't take the bait but plunged ahead with her concern. "He knows some first aid and I told him what happened to you in the ocean. He says you could have had some oxygen deprivation."

Oxygen deprivation. Lack of air. Hallucinations? It made sense.

"No, none of that." Thankfully it was the truth.

"No, she doesn't." Misty said to her hunk. She came back on the line. "That's a good sign, he says."

Oh, thank God, Misty's date was on her side. "I told you, you didn't have to worry. Now go have fun."

"What are you doing now?"

"Come on, already, miss worrywart."

"Cat, indulge me."

"Just had a shower, checked my equipment and now I'm heading off to bed."

"Good. Good. Sleep will be good for you."

"Go, will you? Have fun."

"All right. Stay safe. Kiss. Kiss." And then she disconnected.

"Thank you," Catalina breathed and slapped her cell onto the bathroom counter, clutched her towel to her breasts and padded into her bedroom.

Her room was her sanctuary and with her RV slide-out, she gained an extra three feet of walking space. The room was decorated in brown hues, and she had a small, flat-screen TV up on the wall beside one of her two windows. Normally she would roll into bed and watch the news or a movie, but tonight she was too tired to do any of that.

Flipping on the bedside light, she dropped her towel with the full intention of slipping beneath the covers but froze as she glanced at herself in the full-length mirror on her closet door.

"What in the world?"

She moved closer to the mirror and gazed at the body art on her back. The octopus design and its tentacles stretching sexily up her spine looked the same, yet...they looked different too. The coloring seemed more vibrant than she remembered. And she swore the tentacles appeared...larger? More swollen? Longer than she remembered them and so unbelievably lifelike. If she stared hard enough, she could swear they even moved ever so slightly.

Catalina swallowed back the round of anxiety threatening to pummel her. Why would her tattoos move? And why was her skin so pink and flushed? Yeah, she'd had a shower, and it had been hot, but her skin appeared to be softer, as if it were new.

Okay, Cat. Too much sun today and she was just tired. *Yeah, that's it. Tired.* Maybe she'd gotten too much sun out on the beach *and* lack of oxygen when she'd gone under the water. Perfectly good explanations.

Relief whispered through her. Yeah, maybe she'd had too much sun yesterday too. Too much driving the day before in her hurry to get to California. She'd pushed herself hard getting to her reserved RV campsite. Then yesterday and this afternoon she and Misty had caught up with each other's lives since seeing each other. Of course, that's why she'd been zoning out. Those had to be the reasons.

She blew out a tense breath and opened the nearest window wider to allow more of a breeze to enter the warm room. The gently lapping waves as they hugged the beach about twenty feet away soothed her. From this angle, she got the perfect view of the ocean and the huge, white, full moon sitting on the horizon. Her heart picked up speed as she saw that same houseboat anchored about a mile out. The one she'd seen earlier, right after...

Heat seared through her as she remembered the tender strokes of tentacles touching her flesh then grabbing her nipples. The intoxicating way a tentacle had slipped into her vagina, another plunging into and filling her ass to perfection. Her mouth being impaled.

She blew out an erratic breath. Had someone from that boat attacked her? Maybe someone wearing a tentacle suit or something?

Okay, now that was a crazy idea. She just needed to go to sleep and forget. But as she climbed beneath her sheets, she couldn't forget the delightful green eyes of Calder, or how being around him this morning had made her fantasize about him. And then thinking he'd been a tentacle guy or whatever the hell he had been. Nor could she forget that awesome orgasm she'd experienced while being triple penetrated.

No, she certainly couldn't forget. She didn't even want to.

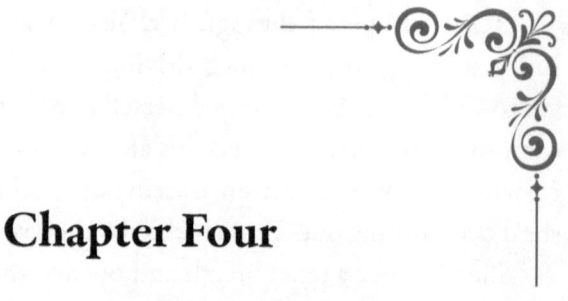

Chapter Four

Surprise washed over Catalina as she stared at the houseboat anchored in slip thirteen. This was Calder's boat? She looked at the receipt she'd found with Calder's credit card. Yes, slip thirteen. Gazing back at the houseboat she frowned as unease crept through her. It looked exactly like the one she'd seen anchored offshore last night. Actually, it was identical.

"Hello! Calder! Are you home?" she called out as she stood on the dock. A small gangplank led to a one-foot-high chrome railing with steps onto the boat deck. If he had the gangplank out, then maybe he'd either left or was waiting for his girlfriend to arrive? Or perhaps his girlfriend had spent the night and left?

Knowing she shouldn't be reacting to those questions, she couldn't stop the uncomfortable frisson of jealousy zipping inside her. Should she board?

She gazed around at the neighboring, colorful boats. All of them were smaller than his. There were sailboats, yachts and large fishing boats, but no one appeared for her to ask whether he was home or not.

Well, she was already here so she may as well take a look around. Maybe he'd come back? Walking up the gangplank, she stepped over the railing and descended onto the polished, wooden deck.

"Hello, Calder? Are you free?"

No answer.

Huh? Now what?

Most of the cabin was comprised of windows, but they were frosted white so she couldn't see inside. Maybe he was sleeping? Perhaps he was toast after a night of hot sex with that girlfriend he loved so much, he'd commissioned Catalina to tattoo tentacles on him and his cock.

Oh Cat, quit thinking this way. Despite not wanting to react, a bubble of irritation made her catch her breath. She was being silly over all this. Too emotional over a man she'd met less than twenty-four hours ago. For her, this sappy kind of attitude was totally out of character. Usually, she enjoyed being alone with her own company. But since meeting Calder, she felt different. Nervous. Needy for him. Needy for a man who was already taken.

Oh God! Cat! Stop all this whining. Knock on the door and, if he's home, hand him the credit card or at least slip it beneath the door.

She better just knock first. At the door, she noticed a cute, brass, heart-shaped knocker. The metal was cool to the touch as she lifted it and brought it down several times. The clack was loud enough she swore everyone in the marina would hear and come looking. Thankfully no one did. And neither did Calder.

Tension embraced her as she waited anxiously for a reply. Nothing.

Okay, on to plan B. Slip the card beneath the door. But first, she had to make sure the door was locked. It wouldn't do for her to slip the card beneath the door if it was unlocked and someone other than Calder came along, found it and used it. Not good.

Okay, so...

Twisting the handle, she was surprised to find it unlocked. She opened the door and inhaled the coffee-scented, cool air breezing against her face. Peeking inside the semi-bright interior, she instantly liked the modern décor of the combination living room kitchenette. The walls were white, frosted glass. A flat-screen TV was mounted on a beam. The floors were a warm-brown, wood-planked vinyl. Two comfortable-looking, dark-brown sofas sat opposite each other with a cushioned coffee table between them. The kitchenette consisted of four black metal chairs bolted into the floor, situated two on each side of an icy-white, faux-granite countertop and stainless-steel sink. He had an electric cook stove on top of the counter and cabinets for storage beneath the sink. Steam rose from a full, glass carafe inside the coffeemaker. Hence, the coffee smell.

From somewhere to the stern of the boat came the distant splash of someone showering. Calder? Excitement raced through her.

He was in the shower. That's why he hadn't answered. He hadn't heard her knock.

Okay, so she would just leave the card and a note. She needed a pen. But she could find no pen. Or paper. Come to think of it, it appeared as if he didn't use this place much. It was way too clean and orderly.

She could take a quick look around, perhaps down the hallway? But she really shouldn't go there. She'd never been in a luxury houseboat before, and the shower was still running. He wouldn't even have to know she was snooping around. Perhaps one little peek around? Surely it wouldn't hurt.

She entered the hallway and immediately found the bathroom. *Sweet mercy!* The door to the bathroom was wide open. She stood right there as the water turned off and the misted shower door slid open.

He stepped out of the shower.

Something...a tremble of wicked lust, a shimmer of intense need, whatever it was had her frozen to the spot as her gaze caressed every, solid muscle rippling across his wide chest.

Wow! The man was built just as great on top as below his waist. Tanned muscles bulged in his upper arms as he grabbed the dark-brown body towel from the bar just outside the shower door. He hadn't seen her yet. She could probably make her escape without being noticed, but then she caught sight of his semi-erect cock. Big. Juicy. Long. Oh, a very long cock.

Had she actually tattooed him? Had he really been this big when she'd done him?

Another sweet shiver of awareness coursed through her as she imagined him making love to her. Her cheeks flamed as he froze, his gaze snapping to her face.

Shit.

Caught.

"I'm so sorry. I mean... I knocked. I really am so sorry." *He really should wrap that towel around his waist.* He didn't. *Oh, yummy man.* She should look away at least. She just couldn't.

"Don't be sorry." His voice melted wonderfully over her senses. "I'm actually glad you came...by. I wanted to talk to you about something important."

The last word was spoken in a deeper tone, and he grabbed her full attention. Not that he didn't already have it. Just now her brain suddenly seemed to be kicking in and overriding her body urges to mate with him.

She blinked in surprise. *Mate?* Okay, sex. Yeah, she meant sex.

"Oh, you're probably worried about your credit card."

He frowned. Obviously, he didn't know what she was talking about.

"I found it in my bathroom," she explained. "You dropped it. I phoned and left a message. I guess you haven't checked them..."

"I just came back from my jog." He wrapped the towel around his narrow waist, hiding his scrumptious cock from her view. Frustration suddenly rocked her. Oh man, she wanted to see it again.

The disappointment disintegrated as he came closer. She could smell him. Clean, fresh, sex-on-a-stick man. She tried to remember the last time she'd had sex, but she came up blank. *That long, huh?*

His hair was wet, dark and drippy. Droplets of water sluiced along his neck and the curves of his big, broad shoulders.

Have mercy! She'd never been so aware of how beads of water looked really erotic rolling down a man's flesh.

"So, that's the only reason you came over? To return my card?" he prodded.

Mischief twinkled in his stormy eyes, and she found herself kind of relaxing. Okay, not really relaxing. Just not so nervous.

"Well, I guess I missed your ugly mug," she teased.

"Ugly, eh?"

Her tummy fluttered as he grinned.

"Very," she giggled.

Suddenly his grin exploded into a full-fledged, deep-from-the-chest laugh, and she realized all too late his intention as he ripped the towel off his waist and snapped one end of it at her.

She turned away from him and the towel bit painfully against her ass. Before he could snap it again, she was racing down the hallway into his bedroom. Laughing, she ran to the other side of his bed, bringing it between the two of them.

His cock bobbed as he snapped the towel across the bed at her.

"Missed!" She giggled. Gosh, how quickly she'd become so happy. So at ease. So riveted to his tentacle-tattooed cock.

He must have seen her interest, because the happiness faded from his face and serious intent shifted into his eyes.

"I won't miss next time, Cat," he said softly.

Her heart pounded with excitement as he strolled around the bed, his lethal towel in his hand, poised to strike her again. It seemed as if he expected her to be an easy victim to his whipping, in the confident way he walked toward her, but she bolted. She jumped onto the firm mattress and before she could scramble to the other side and race for freedom, a hot, very strong arm wrapped around her waist. He pulled her back toward him, and she lost her balance. She went sailing through the air, only to drop onto the bed, right on her back.

He didn't waste any time. He braced his big body over hers, his bare chest mere inches from her breasts, his arms straddling her shoulders as his legs effectively pinned hers down. He lowered his head until he was only inches away.

"Do you take back what you said about my mug being ugly?" he asked.

His minty-fresh breath caressed her nostrils, and the sweet tips of his lips were curling upward ever so slightly. Obviously, his teasing mood had returned.

She swallowed, realizing what a naughty position they were in.

"Make me take it back," she whispered.

His eyes twinkled with wicked intent. "What's the *real* reason you came over, Cat?"

He didn't wait for an answer, and she held her breath as his head lowered. He was about to kiss her.

"No, don't," she commanded as realization caved in all her arousal. The man had a girlfriend!

The two words seemed to hit him like a bucket of cold water. He tensed, his eyes opening wide in surprise and with questions.

"Your girlfriend wouldn't like it."

He blinked in confusion. "Girlfriend? What girlfriend?"

Oh my God! What kind of a man was he? He'd forgotten her already.

Anger roared through her, and she grabbed his upper arms, ignoring the erotic way his muscles rippled beneath her fingertips. Oh, his poor girlfriend.

"Let me up!" she demanded as more anger rushed through her when he didn't budge.

He just frowned and breathed hard as he stared down at her. He didn't like not getting his own way.

"I don't have a girlfriend."

"Yeah, right. How quickly he forgets his girlfriend."

To her irritation, his smile returned. "Are you jealous?"

"You're a creep." She shouldn't anger him, especially in this vulnerable position, lying beneath him and totally at his mercy. But she couldn't help it. She was so pissed off at the moment she literally saw red.

He laughed as if he had just been told a hilarious joke. She should slap him. She really should. As if he was guessing her thoughts, he shook his head.

"Don't you dare, my little tentacle-fetish vixen."

"Screw you."

"Actually, I'd like to screw you, but since I have a girlfriend—"

"I thought you just said—"

"I really don't have one."

"Yesterday, you said—"

"I lied."

He is lying. Don't believe him. He has a girlfriend, and he wants to fuck you and that's why he is saying different. But call her stupid, her instincts told her to believe him.

"Why lie?"

Sadness flashed in his eyes. "It's complicated. I should have told you the truth the moment I knew who you were."

What the hell was he talking about?

But the sadness quickly turned to unmistakable desire. "But since I didn't, you've caught me in a lie, literally, with my pants down."

"Off," she corrected. And suddenly the luscious, hot imprint of his quickly growing shaft pressed against her inner thigh. "Why lie to me about that?"

"I saw you in your RV and I wanted to meet you. I visited your site and realized by your drawings and the pics of tats on your site gallery that you have a tentacle fetish. So, I came up with the story of getting my cock tattooed to meet you."

"You're crazy." Gosh, how insane to go to such lengths just to meet her. "You could have asked me to go out for coffee. That's how most people get to know each other."

"Would you have?"

Cat shrugged. Probably not. She was a loner and preferred to stay that way. Or at least she had until now.

"So, there you have it. And now I'm going to kiss you," he warned. And she instantly recognized the arousal flowing in his eyes.

Before she could mount a protest and ask more questions, his moist, warm lips melted firmly over her mouth, and she was lost in a swirl of exquisite sensations.

"He's mine," an inner voice whispered somewhere deep within her. *"All mine."*

He kissed her hard, wrenching flames of sensuality from her core, drawing them out of her and wrapping them around her like an erotic shield.

Gosh! He sure knew how to kiss.

She opened her mouth to him and his tongue shot inside and dueled with hers. The intense impact of him slipping inside of her was indescribable. She wanted more. Needed more.

He kissed her mouth, sometimes sipping gently, other times fusing over her hard and strong. She couldn't stop the guttural moans of arousal coming from inside her chest. He tasted sweet, sexy and just damned good.

As they kissed, an erotic fire seared into her. She couldn't think about anything else but the two of them, tangled on the bed, his mouth making love to hers. Finally, when he drew away, he cursed softly beneath his breath.

"You are so beautiful. So exquisitely beautiful. I never thought I would find a mate as perfect as you," he said.

She opened her eyes and blinked up at him. She was unable to speak, but she sure did love the intoxicating way his gaze trapped her beneath him.

"Your kisses turn me on so bad," he whispered. His mouth descended again, but this time he kissed the length of her neck with such tender, erotic kisses she was creaming in her panties with every touch of his lips against her flesh.

Oh yeah, they were mates. Perfect mates.

He kissed along her collarbone and when he reached her blouse his mouth pulled hard until buttons were flying. He growled when he met her bra.

"Let me—"

But he ignored her. He climbed off her and, to her surprise, grabbed the middle of her bra and ripped it down the middle, allowing her breasts to spill free to his view.

She swallowed as he smiled. "Exquisite breasts. I don't want you to hide them from me. Don't wear a bra anymore," he demanded.

He sat on the bed beside her and, dipping his head, he gently kissed one nipple and then the other with tender, butterfly kisses. Her breasts swelled and her nipples beaded until she swore they were as hard as two pebbles.

She would have told him where he could go, concerning her not wearing a bra. After all, she barely knew the guy. But hey, arguments were for later. Her thoughts drifted away as he began kissing a line of fire along her belly. When he reached her jeans, he growled again. The guttural response made the blood hum through her veins.

His breath grew quicker and hers joined his as he undid the clasp on her jeans. She helped him pull her pants down and he drew them off and hurled them somewhere in the room. His dark-green eyes glittered as he ripped her panties in half and folded the cloth to the sides. Eagerness and anticipation roared through her as he stood along the foot of the bed, over her legs.

She cried out in utter surprise as he lowered himself between her thighs, his shoulders widening her legs as he nestled between. Hot breath sprayed against her pussy, and she couldn't believe he was actually considering going down on her. No man had *ever* put his head down *there*.

She tensed as his tongue slipped between her pussy lips, and she jerked involuntarily as he licked a hard line right up the middle of her parted labia and onto her sensitive clit and off. He did it again. And again.

Whoa! Awesome! The pleasure was indescribable as he licked and lapped and sipped her cream from her body. He brought her close to orgasm so many times she couldn't count them. She wanted to scream. To cry. To pound her fists on his back, but instead she just lay there, enjoying the pleasure, her hands fisted in the comforter on his bed. She could only breathe through the unique sensations threatening to consume her. It was almost as if she'd experienced sex in this instinctual way with him before. Almost as if she were down at the bottom of the ocean again, her body filled with tentacles as she orgasmed over and over.

Somewhere deep in the recesses of her mind, she remembered that happening. Orgasms and lust and love emanating from the other who'd fucked her in the ocean. The one she'd thought was Calder. But that idea was crazy. Simply crazy. She shut off that insane part of her brain and just enjoyed the intense way Calder's hands gripped her hips as he held her down and feasted on her pussy.

When she swore, she could take his exquisite torture no longer, he finally let go of her. A quick rip of foil followed. Protection. She'd forgotten about condoms in the heat of the moment. He slipped a condom onto his huge shaft, and she cried out as he climbed over her. She grabbed his shoulders, her fingers curling over his flesh and digging into his sinewy muscles as she pulled him down on her. His legs aligned on top of hers, the huge, hot tip of his cock head slid into her wet vagina.

She shuddered as he entered her. Cried out as his tentacle-tattooed cock slid deep and hard, his huge girth spreading her tight muscles as he impaled her. His chest pressed her breasts, embracing them. His harsh mouth, fused with hers, cut off her cries. She tightened her vagina around his cock, welcoming him, loving his fullness and the heat.

She moaned as he withdrew and plunged into her. It was a heavy and powerful thrust that had the headboard of his bed grating against the wall. He penetrated her with such wicked speed the impact left her delirious with arousal. He withdrew and powered into her again.

He fucked her with hard strokes. Fucked her until the pleasure overrode her senses and she exploded in a frenzy. It was agonizing ecstasy as spasms rushed through her like a drug. She was flying high. Bucking beneath him, accepting him and loving him. He thrust harder, stealing her breath away with his furious pistoning and wonderful kisses, and within seconds she fell into her very own awesome pleasure world.

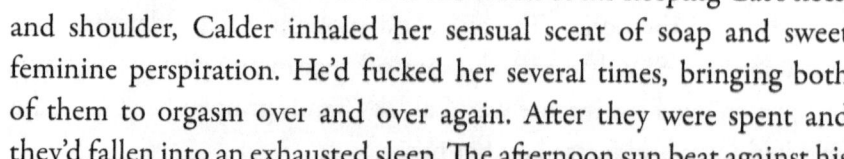

NUZZLING HIS CHIN INTO the crook of his sleeping Cat's neck and shoulder, Calder inhaled her sensual scent of soap and sweet feminine perspiration. He'd fucked her several times, bringing both of them to orgasm over and over again. After they were spent and they'd fallen into an exhausted sleep. The afternoon sun beat against his white-frosted windows and with all their sexual exercises, his bedroom was getting quite hot. But he didn't want to leave her side to go and turn on the air conditioner and he didn't want to wake her either.

Although he really should. She probably had customers today. They would be pissed off she hadn't canceled or shown up. She would be pissed off he hadn't woken her. But he'd deal with that later, when the time came. Right now, he just wanted to keep inhaling her comfortable warmth and watch her tentacle tattoos as they ebbed and flowed in vibrant colors with her every breath.

She was in the process of her change now. In a matter of days, she would permanently be an Octoposeidon like himself. She would be a shapeshifter. Human by day and part-human, part-octopus by night.

He only hoped she didn't lose her sanity when she discovered the truth. His species, direct descendants of the god Poseidon and his mating with an octopus, were always near extinction. The males outnumbered the females by about a thousand to one. This was why males who were lucky enough to find a mate were so territorial and aggressive against other males, whether in human or Octoposeidon form. Understandably mutations had occurred, when a human was unable to accept the change and insanity ensued. If that happened, it would be up to him to kill her to protect their species. If humans ever discovered his kind existed, the humans would most likely hunt them down to extinction, just as they had done to so many other species.

Calder reached up and ran his fingers through the strands of her silky hair. No, she would accept her identity. She would not go insane or into denial. She couldn't. He was already in love with her and if he couldn't get her to fall in love with him, then surely, he'd die of loneliness.

Chapter Five

Catalina awoke to the cool breeze brushing against her hot skin. Blinking, she winced at the muted sunshine, streaming in compliments of the frosted windows on three sides of the bedroom. Stretching out on the bed, she smiled at how absolutely wonderful she felt. So satisfied and happy. Very happy. The man certainly did know how to pleasure a woman.

Calder was definitely experienced. She'd have to question him regarding his past. Where he came from. What kind of work he did. His hobbies.

Suddenly she wanted to know everything about him. Usually, she was so cautious in picking bed partners. Okay, so she was way overcautious and that's why she'd only slept with four guys in her life excluding Calder. The others had been mediocre in the lovemaking department, mainly catering to their own needs. Oh, they'd made a show of trying to arouse her, but in the end, they stopped when they'd satisfied themselves.

But Calder... Catalina trembled as the cool air met her sizzling memories. Calder just kept fucking her and raining orgasms on her. She'd had no idea she could climax so many times. The most she'd ever climaxed was twice and that had been by her own hand.

She licked her lips. They were tender from his intense kisses. Tender and bruised. She loved the confident way he'd kissed her body too. His mouth had made love to her skin with those butterfly kisses. And that tongue... What an erotic tongue in the way he could wrap it around her nipple like a tentacle, latching on and pulling and tugging.

She blinked in wonder. Could a man really do that with a tongue? He was quite talented with it. She wouldn't mind having a repeat performance. Which led her to the question of where was he anyway?

A flowery scent sifted beneath her nostrils, and she turned her head to find a beautiful, yellow daffodil with a pretty, sky-blue ribbon wrapped around its green stem. A small note hung off one end of the ribbon. Turning onto her side, she reached out and held the note between her fingers.

Follow the petals. Love, Calder

The petals? What in the world? She sat up and gazed around. There, on his side of the bed, strewn all over the rumpled sheets, were yellow daffodil petals. When she rolled over, she spied a row of petals on the floor. They led to the sliding doors at the back of the bedroom.

Huh. She hadn't even noticed those doors earlier when she'd come in. They were frosted white glass just like the walls.

Cool. She pushed herself out of bed and slid open one of the doors. Hot air blew against her naked body as she looked out onto the sparkling, blue-green ocean. So beautiful. When she gazed to her right, she noticed the shadow of a boat anchored in the slip beside Calder's houseboat. To her left floated a row of colorful boats of all varieties. Her cheeks grew warm, wondering if his neighbors had heard any of her cries as she'd climaxed. She shook her head in disbelief.

She'd just had sex with a man she'd known for barely twenty-four hours. Come to think of it, since meeting him yesterday she really hadn't been herself. She'd fantasized about him to the point where she'd actually lost blocks of time.

Sex, good. Memory loss, not good.

He wanted her to follow the daffodil petals, and she would, but just long enough to tell him she needed a shower. Maybe he'd join her?

Her cheeks flamed at that thought. Sex with a man in a shower. Nope, definitely never done that before.

She discovered a light-blue, terrycloth robe neatly folded on a chair. She grabbed it, put it on and slipped onto the back deck into the hot sunshine.

Immediately she wished for a swimsuit so she could dive right off the boat and into the cool, blue waters. From nearby, seemingly from the roof area of Calder's houseboat, sounds of nature music saturated the air. It was low, but she could make out the lapping of water and birds singing. It had a calming effect on her.

Gazing at the petals, she followed the line of yellow to the narrow side until it went up some metal stairs that led to the roof area. Smiling, she padded quietly up the stairs, and as she came toward the top, amazement splashed through her in exciting waves.

He had a miniature swimming pool up here on his freaking roof! On one of the several patio chairs sat the culprit of the music, a radio. And doing the breaststroke in the crystal-clear water of the swimming pool was Calder.

Oh my. He was naked.

When he spied her, he smiled and did a quick wave. "Come on in. The water is fantastic," he shouted.

"I don't have a swimsuit," she called back, clutching the robe tighter around her as she gazed at the nearby assembly of houseboats, yachts and sailboats.

"Skinny dip!" He laughed.

She couldn't do that! Could she? Tremors of excitement hummed through her.

"Don't worry. It's a nudist area. It's okay!"

Nudist area? Oh my gosh!

Getting naked with a man in his bedroom was one thing. Getting naked out in the open where anyone and everyone could be watching? It wasn't her style. But then, she'd never been to a nudist beach or nudist area. Now if everyone else was naked...oh! Why not? He'd already seen her in her birthday-bathing suit, so to speak. So yeah, why not?

In a rush of courage, she dropped the security of the robe and cannonballed into the water. The ear-splitting splash hit her at the same time the cool water embraced her hot body.

Breathtaking. Beautiful. So, refreshing.

She swam beneath the surface, her arms and legs wonderfully light and fluid. She could stay down here in this refreshment forever. But too soon, she needed to come up for air. Inhaling the fresh, salty, ocean air, she allowed it to fill her lungs.

She'd jumped into the deep end as her feet didn't touch the ground, so she treaded water. And she found Calder swimming right in front of her. He was smiling, grinning from ear to ear as he gazed at her.

His obvious happiness was contagious, seeping into her every nerve and fiber.

"I guess I should have asked if you can swim."

"Too late!" She laughed.

"Here I was all prepared to give you mouth to mouth."

Giggles burst through her. Oh, a kiss would be nice.

"Ummm...mouth to mouth. I like that. How about we pretend I'm drowning?" She laughed.

He licked a bead of water off his upper lip as he swam closer. Leaning in, his cool mouth breezed against hers, soft and pure. Delicate sensations rippled through her.

"You taste good," he said, after he broke the tender kiss.

"You taste better."

"I want to make love to you again. Here. Now."

"I'd like that." Oh boy, she really would!

With a nod, he indicated she should follow him. She did, but she kept her gaze glued to his tight ass as he swam toward the shallow end of the pool.

"Condoms are ready," he said as he lifted the lid off a small, pocket-sized, silver box he'd set on a ladder step.

"Let me," she whispered, wanting to see his cock again. To touch it and explore the power of his flesh between her fingers.

He nodded and handed her a package before moving the box onto the deck. Muscles bulged in his tanned arms as he hoisted himself up into a seated position on the edge of the pool near the ladder. She became mesmerized by how the water ran in rivulets down his form. Gosh, he was a perfectly shaped man. Wide shoulders, lean torso and such a yummy, long and swollen, tentacle-tattooed cock.

Warm cream seeped into her suddenly quivering pussy. She remembered how awesome she'd felt when his mouth had fused over her. Her breath quickened as an idea came to her. Slipping the package containing the condom onto the ladder step, she grabbed his knees. Surprise burst in his eyes as she widened his legs. She began to tremble at the hot, lusty look in his eyes.

"I'm going to do to you what you did to me earlier," she whispered.

His gaze drew to her mouth as she licked her lips. Tension rippled through his body, the muscles in his chest flexing and his breath quickening as she dropped onto her knees in the pool. The water rose, cool and caressing against the tender tips of her nipples. She settled between his thighs, let go of his knees and palmed his big shaft with one hand and, with the other, began gently squeezing his balls.

He inhaled sharply. "You look good down there between my legs, Catalina," he whispered.

He leaned forward. Reaching out, he cupped her breasts, caressing them in the same gentle rhythm as she did his scrotum. He groaned and she answered with a sultry moan of her own. It felt good just the two of them, leisurely massaging each other. She didn't even care if anyone around was watching them. It seemed as if it was just the two of them in the whole world. It was the same kind of encounter she'd experienced last night while she'd been under the water. Being wanted, needed and loved. She should mention to him what had happened to her last night. But she simply didn't want to break the mood. So, she kept quiet, loving the neat carnal sensations embracing her.

Leaning over, she licked the smooth, hot tip of Calder's swollen cock head. Closing her eyes, she moaned as his fingers pinched and tugged at her nipples. They quickly grew hot and hard, blossoming into tight pebbles.

Having a man's cock in her mouth was different and exciting. She liked it. She'd have to do this more often with Calder because from the way his eyes were squeezed tight and the awesome way he was rubbing her nipples, he really enjoyed it.

His hips arched upward as she devoured more of his swollen flesh into her mouth. He was solid, powerful and unbelievably big.

"Suck, baby, suck," he hissed. His fingers became harsher, more desperate on her nipples, making her breasts swollen and her pussy warm with cream. She brought him deeper into her mouth, until his cock hit the back of her throat, before she sucked around his flesh.

He let out a gurgled cry. The rough shout was like a fever slipping into her bloodstream. She sucked harder, loving the array of guttural groans erupting from deep inside his chest.

She slid her hand off his scrotum and it joined the other one, embracing his shaft, holding him as she brought him in and out of her mouth, moving fast and quick, slurping his rigid flesh until his groans grew even hoarser and she imagined him pistoning into her.

He got the same idea, for suddenly he emitted out a frustrated growl, let go of her nipples and warned her he was jumping into the water. With his arousal and anticipation roaring through her own bloodstream, she released his cock and gave him the room he needed to slip into the water in front of her.

"I need to take you now, baby," he growled as he grabbed her by her hips and turned her around, so she was braced by the wall of the pool. The intense way his eyes flared with lust had her reaching up and holding his rigid muscles as he slipped his big cock into her.

He moved quickly against her, his hard body melting with hers for a split second as he impaled her, then leaving as he withdrew. He stroked into her effectively and efficiently, angling his cock so he teased her sensitive clit every time he thrust into her. Within seconds, she was gasping into a climax that slammed into her like a storm.

She quivered as he made love to her. Her body trembling with his every firm, delicious thrust. Her aroused cries snapped through the hot afternoon air and mingled with the shrieks of seagulls. It was a beautiful music as he just kept pumping faster and harder. He brought several breathtaking orgasms out of her, his lips eventually sliding over hers, covering her mouth and catching her cries.

Only after he'd succeeded in wrenching four climaxes out of her, did he finally cry out in a hoarse shout, and she shuddered wonderfully as his warm seed shot deep inside of her. And only then did she realize they hadn't used protection. But it didn't matter. Yes, she might be naïve in thinking this way, but they fit together so perfectly. They belonged together and they'd just shared such beautiful sex. Nothing bad could come from such beauty. No way, and at that moment she wanted to hold onto this happiness forever and she wanted this man in her heart. Always.

CALDER DIDN'T WANT to withdraw from her. He loved being buried inside her pussy. Loved just standing in the water, beneath the warm sunlight, rhythmically moving their hips to the soft music whispering over them from the radio. But he needed to leave her. Just for the night. When he turned back into his human form, he'd be here again in the morning.

"Cat," he whispered as the golden rays of sunlight quickly disappeared all around them.

Shit. It was later than he thought. A new sense of urgency split into him. He *needed* to get her out of here.

"Don't go," she whispered against his warm mouth as he tried to pull out of her. "We didn't use protection," he replied. "But I'll do right by you, I promise, and I'm not carrying any diseases. I don't usually do this myself. I usually know a woman much, much longer."

He hoped she believed him because it was the truth. He was clean and he'd never had unprotected sex while in his human shape. But with his desirable Catalina he'd just lost all self-control.

"A gentleman of honor," she chuckled and kissed his mouth. Damn she knew how to kiss. Her mouth was warm and fit so wonderfully over his, and her kisses just made him so happy and heady and aroused.

His cock tightened and hardened inside of her. He had to stop this before it went any farther. Daylight was burning quickly, and he had to get ready for his change.

"I...I have to go to work. I'm on the night shift at a marina," he explained.

SHE BLINKED AS SUDDEN realization slammed into her. Work? *Oh shit!* She'd totally forgotten she'd been booked solid with clients today.

Damn," she spat as he pulled out. He chuckled as he let go of her hips.

"I didn't think you'd be that disappointed," he grinned at her and her belly did a really cool somersault. Yep, she really liked the way this guy made her feel.

"I'm not. But I totally will never live this down."

Guilt gripped her as she followed him out of the pool.

"Live this down? What? Are you afraid my neighbors will talk about my fucking you in the pool?" He chuckled and handed her a white towel. She grabbed it and quickly wrapped it around her waist and then pulled it up under her armpits, tucking in the folds.

"No, my clients. I have a full day. How in God's name could I ever forget them? This has never happened to me before. So many crazy things have happened since I met you."

"Good things, I hope?"

She couldn't help but nod as she stared into his mesmerizing green eyes. Gosh, she could just literally fall into those beautiful eyes and stay there forever.

"So, I guess we're both late for work?" he asked as he switched off his radio and picked it up. Her breath quickened again as his stiff cock bobbed up and down as he opened a nearby steel cabinet and placed the radio inside. Suddenly her lips burned for him. She wanted them pressed against his mouth again. To feel his confident warmth slide over her lips and drown in the lash of his eager tongue pressed against hers.

"I thought of that earlier, but I didn't want to lose you," he said as he headed toward the staircase. She quickly followed and they descended to the main deck.

Yeah, but he certainly seemed as if he could stand losing her now. Why did she get the feeling he wanted to brush her off? Gosh, what if she was pregnant and he wanted nothing to do with her? Iciness slithered around her heart. She hadn't just been used, had she? She hadn't just made the biggest mistake of her life, having unprotected sex with a guy she barely knew, did she?

Catalina frowned. She was being an idiot. She'd used him too. Kind of.

Okay, so she was confused. First of all, she'd never had unprotected sex before and she'd certainly never slept with a guy she barely knew. She'd better go home and get some distance. She'd clean up there, because if she stayed here, she'd most likely follow him right into the shower and let him screw her brains out. Again.

Her frown deepened. But she truly wanted to stay here with him.

"We'll see each other tomorrow morning, right?" He turned to her and must have noticed her confusion for he was suddenly cuddling her in his strong, protective embrace, his warm body pressed against hers, his hot breath caressing her cheeks.

Oh yeah, she definitely wanted to stay here and get to know more about him.

"How about I come over for breakfast?" she asked, staring deep into his eyes and wondering if he was falling as hard for her as she was for him. Oh dear, she was being bold. But she liked being bold, especially with him. She wanted him to know she was very interested in him.

"I'll be here bright and early. And I'll have breakfast ready for you by the pool. How's that?" he said against her lips.

"Sounds wonderful." Although she'd much rather spend the night.

"*Distance,*" an inner voice whispered. She needed distance to think about what she'd just allowed to happen. Hot sex. Hot *unprotected* sex.

"Okay, I need to get showered and changed," he whispered and when he let go of her, she felt lost and so alone.

"I'm going to miss you like crazy," he said as he headed out of the bedroom, his voice hoarse and strangled, as if maybe he really was sincere.

A moment later, the shower came on. The overwhelming urge to join him almost won out. But she wasn't acting like herself. She'd never been this needy for a man. Right now, she had to get dressed and she had to leave. Or she swore if she didn't, she'd be here with him forever.

"*Not such a bad idea,*" that naughty inner voice whispered.

CALDER BREATHED A HUGE sigh of relief when he came out of the shower to find Catalina gone. But that relief was short-lived by an ache that carved so deeply into his hearts he wished he had explained to her why he'd needed her gone.

Gazing down at his engorged cock, the colors shimmered bright and vibrant. The warning signs for change. Normally without a tattoo he would have experienced that familiar sense of urgency to head for the ocean before he shifted. But now that he had the tattoo, it was an earlier signal for the upcoming change. It had everything to do with the skin pigmentation readying itself. He wondered if other shifters knew about this. He would have to mention tattoos as signals of the change at their annual convention next year.

Pushing that thought aside, he prepared to get his houseboat out of here and onto the ocean and into a secluded spot as quickly as possible. Then he could safely slip into the water to await his change.

Glancing at the clock in his bedroom, he realized he had just enough time to clear the marina, anchor his boat at some private bay and jump into the water. He didn't want to cut it as close as last night.

As he slipped on his swim pants and headed to the pilothouse, the familiar pounding of blood rushed through his veins. The tattoo had given him a good five-minute leeway. That wasn't too much time, but for Octoposeidons who needed to get away from humans in a hurry, a shimmering tattoo might make all the difference in alerting them to the approaching change.

Moments later, he maneuvered his houseboat out of the marina, and ten minutes after that, he'd settled into a secluded inlet up the coast. Just in time too, because his body was beginning to go cold and his limbs were softening to the point where his legs were shaky, and he could barely stand.

It was almost dark outside, and the change was beginning. No sooner had he hit the water, did the urge to swim hit. He resisted that urge and waited until it became hard to breathe the air. Then he slid his head under, inhaling, allowing the oxygenated water to sluice deep into his newly formed gills.

Strength quickly fused through his body and his flesh flowed and ebbed as he began to reshape. His bones disintegrated as his new form took hold. The transformation barely hurt. More so in the beginning, but his brain and nerve endings had gotten used to it and readjusted easily now. Females were luckier and didn't experience the pain as males. Something to do with their hormones.

Soon, his tentacles slid back and forth in front of his eyes. His hearing got worse. But that was normal. He didn't really need his hearing down here. His eyes were his guide for seeking food and potential enemies. Propelling himself through the murky darkness, a solemn loneliness crashed through him.

He missed Catalina. He missed her like crazy.

"OH MY GOD! WHERE HAVE you been?" Misty cried as Catalina rounded the corner of her RV and found Misty sitting on the picnic table just outside Cat's door. Her friend jumped off the table and gave her a huge hug before pulling away and staring at her.

"What's up? Why have you not been answering my calls?" She didn't wait for Cat to explain before she headed over to the door and snapped two separate sheets of paper out of the door jamb. She waved the papers at Cat.

"Two customers left notes saying they were here for their tats, but you weren't. This isn't like you, Cat. You never miss work. At least never when you've been here. Did you have another episode like the ones you had yesterday?"

Her friend's worried expression truly made Cat feel guilty.

"Everything is fine," she reassured. Oh boy, she was very energized, despite all that sex today, and she was famished. "Truly fine. Come on inside. I'll flip on my air con. Have you eaten anything yet?"

Misty shook her head. "I couldn't eat a thing not knowing if you were okay or not."

"Well, now you can eat, sweetie. Come on in." She curled her hand into Misty's and, after unlocking her door, she pulled her friend up the stairs and they went inside.

"I DON'T KNOW HOW YOU survive when I'm on the road, Miss." Catalina laughed as she set two plates filled with seafood salad onto the small bench table that doubled for her tattoo foyer and sat opposite Misty who poured them two glasses of red wine.

"Contrary to popular belief, I do worry about you." She reached out and placed her hands over Cat's, squeezing gently. "Um, that's why I call you every day, remember?" Misty asked softly.

Catalina laughed. "How could I forget?"

"So...?" Curiosity sparkled in Misty's eyes. "You missed work. You say everything is fine. You look like a fox who just swallowed the canary. It must mean...hmm, the man with the tentacle tattoo?"

Cat feigned ignorance as she stabbed her fork into a piece of crab. She was actually starving tonight and the seafood salad she'd made early this morning and stashed in her refrigerator for supper was coming in very handy.

"And...so...what did you two do today? It must have been something swanky if you didn't even bother to let your clients know their appointments had been canceled."

Guilt assailed her yet again. She needed to call them and apologize. She stabbed another forkful of seafood and shoved it into her mouth.

Delightful salty flavors exploded against her taste buds, and she moaned softly at the array of sensations bursting over her tongue.

"Hmm, in the way you're eating..." Misty's eyes widened in shock and then excitement.

"Obviously you haven't eaten all day. Did you two...?" She raised her eyebrows up and down several times and Cat had to laugh at the intense anticipation flooding through Misty's features.

"Did we what?" Cat couldn't help but tease.

"You know..."

"No, I don't know. No, we didn't eat if that's what you are insinuating." Her cheeks warmed quite a lot as she remembered why they didn't eat. Actually, that wasn't true. They did eat. Each other.

"You had sex!" Misty gasped. This time, she moved to the edge of her seat and squirmed around like an excited child.

With Misty, Cat had never really been embarrassed talking about sex. Actually, she had several friends around the country who were such true friends, even if she saw them once or twice a year for a few weeks, it was as if they'd never been apart. She was lucky she seemed to gravitate toward loyal and concerned friends such as Misty. And she could talk to them about her sex life. Or lack thereof. Until now.

Cat laughed at her friend's surprised reaction. "It's not like it's my first time."

"Oh my God! It must be serious. I mean, you always wait until you know a guy longer before you have sex with him." Her friend frowned. "But it can't be serious. You just met him yesterday and you mentioned a girlfriend."

"He lied about the girlfriend. He doesn't have one."

A deeper frown marred Misty's forehead and her voice softened as if she were suddenly talking to an inexperienced teenager. "Oh no, honey, guys use that line all the time to get a girl into bed."

"I'm going with my gut on this. I believe him."

"You hardly know him. You could get hurt. I don't want you to get hurt."

"I know, but...it just happened and oh my gosh I've never had such good sex. I've *never* had good sex...until this guy. I mean, we were clowning around at his houseboat, and we just fell into bed." She, of course, meant that quite literally. "And after I awoke, we did it in his swimming pool. Just dancing in the pool listening to music, holding each other like it was the most natural thing in the world."

Misty's face broke into a huge smile. "That's wonderful, Cat. I'm so happy for you. When are you meeting him again?"

"In the morning. For breakfast. At his place. By his pool."

"Morning pool sex. Very exciting. Why can't I find hot guys with tentacle tattoos who give great sex?"

This was Cat's clue to take the focus off herself and back to Misty. The poor dear suddenly looked utterly miserable.

"I take it your fireman date didn't go so well?"

"It went down in flames. I cried myself to sleep with my face buried in my pillow."

Sympathy, once again, assailed her. "Oh, Misty. I'm so sorry. You should have called me."

She pouted prettily. "I didn't want to wake you."

"Then I should have kept my mouth shut about Calder. I'm so sorry."

Misty brightened and chased Cat's guilt away. "No, don't be. At least you had a wonderful time with your man. I'm so happy you found a decent guy who gives great sex and, if I may add, a well-hung man."

"I don't know him well enough to say he's decent, but well hung, definitely."

Misty laughed, suddenly out of her momentary funk. Cat sighed in relief as they polished off their salads and wine and Misty began to chat about auditions for acting jobs she had this coming week.

Later that evening, after Misty had left, Catalina called her customers, profusely apologizing, claiming an unexpected family emergency before rescheduling them for next week. She cleared the rest of the week too, moving other customers so she could spend all her time getting to know Calder more.

When she finally fell into bed, her dreams were filled with tentacles and sex and her man with the tentacle tattoo.

Chapter Six

Catalina arrived at Calder's houseboat bright and early the next morning. When she reached the door, she smiled as she found a note taped to the doorknocker. Along with the note was a beautiful red rose with a pretty ribbon wrapped around the stem and tied into a puffy bow.

For my love.

Catalina blinked back the unexpected rush of happy tears that bubbled up inside her.

Love? Was this possible? They'd just met. Yet since meeting him, she'd been thinking of him almost every waking hour, and then dreaming about him as she slept. She entered the houseboat and found it invitingly cool inside. Thankfully, he'd gotten a head start on the hot day. Red rose petals had been dropped along a line that went to the kitchen area. On top of the counter, she found an enormous bowl filled with an array of fruits and chocolate-covered croissants.

Oh man, if he was trying to impress her, it was working. She picked a couple of white plates from a stack beside the bowl and filled them with strawberries, orange slices, watermelon balls and melon chunks. She topped each plate with three sweet-smelling croissants. Her mouth watered and she grabbed the plates and continued following the rose petals, which led down the hall, past the bathroom into his bedroom. She laughed when she spied another note pinned to the back doors.

No clothes allowed my love.

Oh my. He wanted her to go outside and up the stairs naked.

She giggled, suddenly daring and free. Oh yeah, she could handle walking around naked.

Slipping out of her sandals, she placed the two plates on a nearby bureau and slid off her light-blue blouse and accompanying short skirt. Then she removed her powder-blue bra, something she'd still need to chat with Calder about, concerning his remark about him not wanting her to wear a bra. Yeah sure, she would prefer not to wear one either, but her customers might not approve seeing her nipples jutting out against her clothing.

She removed her panties which she then hung over a nearby chair.

A damp, rumpled towel lay on top of the seat, and she shook her head. Didn't Calder know not to just leave damp towels around? They smelled musty in that condition. Lifting the towel with full intention of placing it over a railing to dry, she froze.

On the chair was a woman's swimsuit. Not just any woman's, but her bikini. The one she'd worn a couple of nights ago when she'd been in the ocean and had that weird blackout and dreamed of sex and tentacles and Calder. And after, she'd been naked, her swimsuit gone.

What the hell? Suddenly she was icy cold. How had he gotten her bikini? Was it just a coincidence that he'd fished it out of the water? She picked up her bikini bottoms and top. Dry. Okay, so this was incredibly weird.

CALDER SKIMMED THE top of the pool with a net, making sure every last bug was out. It wouldn't be sexy, having Catalina covered in dead bugs as the two of them swam and fucked in the water. The good thing about having such a large houseboat, it was quite private up here because most of the other boats were smaller and lower. He wasn't one of those men who wanted to be a visual spectacle when kissing and making out with his woman. Just thinking about finally finding his mate had him grinning happily. As he set the net into the nearby locker, he removed the radio and placed it on a chair. Some nice, slow music, like yesterday, along with Catalina, and they'd be all set for some early-morning mating.

His cock throbbed against his swim trunks, and he moaned softly at the idea of taking her again. A sudden ping on the metal stairs had him turning around. His hearts beat faster as she stepped onto the wooden deck, her hands laden with two plates filled with fruit and croissants. He was famished. She was wearing the powder-blue robe again. Her not being naked was okay. She wasn't as bold walking around that way as he was and he found her shyness very cute.

She would eventually get over it. When she shifted, she would have no choice. Octoposeidons preferred to swim without the constraints of clothing. They just swam, ate seafood and fucked. It was a leisurely life.

That is, until a mate became involved. Then their species needed to be on guard for attacking males who would be desperate to mate with a female, especially when her scent drifted along the currents, enticing others back to her. To them. The same could happen when she was in human form. If an Octoposeidon was within twenty miles of a female Octoposeidon, all he'd need to do was sniff the air and follow her scent. But Calder would deal with all that as it happened.

He'd been so excited to see her, at first, he hadn't noticed how pale her face was or how tightly pinched her lips were. Her eyes blazed with a fierceness that was like a punch to his stomach. Alarm raced through him.

"What's wrong?"

She said nothing as she set the plates down on a bolted glass table between a couple of lounge chairs. She untied the sash on her rope and opened it wide. His knees weakened when he saw the bikini. He thought about lying. About pretending it belonged to a neighbor who'd dropped by for a swim. No, that sounded lame. Nudists didn't wear bathing suits.

Shit.

"I can explain," he began.

But she held up her hands for him to remain silent. He did, but his hearts were pounding insanely against his chest as he had hoped to break the news to her slowly. He realized now it had just been wishful thinking he could tell her in a gentle way she was a shifter. Her tattoos were already darkening, swelling and even glimmering, and her flesh appeared supple, fresh and pink as her body began to beautify itself to catch a male.

"Seriously, I can explain."

Doubt flashed in her eyes. "Please, I don't want any lies. At first, I thought, hey, he found the bikini floating in the water and picked it up. But then I got to thinking, why would you pick it up? You didn't know who it belonged to. You certainly would have no idea it belonged to me. Right?"

"Please, just let me explain, Cat."

She shook her head vigorously, became more agitated. "No, no explanations. I think I know what's going on. You saw my website or maybe someone told you about me. You found out I had a tentacle fetish. Okay so you figured, hey, I want my cock tattooed like a tentacle so she'll be turned on and I can fuck her brains out."

"Cat, that's not it."

She laughed. An edge of anger tainted her amusement. Okay, so more than an edge. She was really pissed off.

"So, you got your jollies by exposing yourself to me. Nice hard-on, by the way. I'm glad you got your rocks off. Then I figured you probably must have dropped something in my coffee. Maybe a hallucinogenic, and that's why I don't remember tattooing you, and that's why I had all those other fantasies of you instead. I haven't figured out how you got yourself tattooed, but I sure don't remember doing it."

"Cat, I promise you weren't drugged. You did the tattooing yourself."

"Um sorry, no, I don't believe you. Then somehow the drug went into some kind of lull, and then I became coherent enough to let you go, allow myself to have a bit of normal time with my friend on the beach, until I went into the water, when you somehow grabbed me and I don't know, maybe gave me another shot of whatever you gave me. Then you dragged me into your boat...because I know you were out there. I saw your boat. While I was drugged you removed my bathing suit, attacked me, maybe you noticed people were looking for me and then dumped me back into the water. Am I close?"

"Sweetheart, you're not even close."

"You're an asshole, Calder. If that's what your name even is. You're a freaking mental case who gets off on exposing yourself, drugging your victims and then—"

"That's enough, Cat," he snapped as anger bit into him. He couldn't swallow the thought that she would think such evilness about him.

"I should have known you were too good to be true." Tears glistened in her eyes, and the sight of how unhappy he made her rocked his very foundation.

He may as well be blunt. "Catalina, I'm a shapeshifter."

"You're an idiot. I should report you to the cops."

She made a move to leave, but he grabbed her wrist, hard enough to prevent her from going but, hopefully, not enough to hurt her. She tried to yank herself free, but he held tight.

"Let go of me or I'll scream my fucking head off so much you'll wish you never met me."

"That'll never happen," he soothed.

"You watch me scream."

"I meant I'll never wish I never met you. You're my mate."

She made a strangled gurgle. "Yeah, well, dream on, buddy."

"Cat, please, this isn't the way I wanted to tell you, but I can see I'm running out of time."

Her eyes flared with another round of anger. "Damn right you're running out of time. You probably didn't expect me to catch on so quickly. Now let go of me or you will be sorry."

"Will you promise to hear me out?"

"No. Let go."

"I just need to tell you a couple of things. They'll make sense. Then you will believe me."

He had to tell her the truth. Now. "You've probably already noticed your eyesight is getting sharper. Your tattoo colors are more vibrant. Your skin is getting pinker, softer, more sensitive. Maybe your tattoos are swelling and moving."

She gasped sharply and her eyes widened with recognition. Yes, she'd noticed changes, but then a veil of denial came down and anger splashed into her gaze again. She shook her head as if denying what he'd said was true.

"It means your body is beginning to readjust itself for the change. Watch yourself tonight in the mirror at sunset. Then you'll believe me."

The disbelief and disgust that flashed across her face just about dropped him to his knees.

"Before you go, I need to tell you something else. You're a shapeshifter too. You're an Octoposeidon. Nights we shift into part-octopus, part-human and days we are human. That evening when you lost your bikini, you'd shifted, and I ripped it off you. We made love on the ocean floor before you shifted back again. I brought it onto my boat when I shifted back to human form. That's how it got to my bedroom. I took it out this morning, to smell your scent, because I missed you so much. I forgot to hide it again."

With a strength he didn't realize she was capable of; she yanked her arm free from his grip. Her face flushed red with rage.

"You are fucking insane."

And then she laughed. The stiff way she carried herself as she walked toward the stairs made him once again wish he'd been able to tell her in a more reassuring manner. He'd handled this very badly and he had only himself to blame.

"Cat, please don't go like this. I can explain some more."

"Leave me the hell alone!" she flung over her shoulder. And then she was gone.

"I'M PULLING OUT TONIGHT. Leaving for my next stop." Catalina said to Misty over the phone. She tried like hell to keep the stupid emotional quiver out of her thick voice, but she just couldn't damn well do it.

"But you said you were staying a month, Cat. It's only been a few days. Not even. What gives? Is it the new guy?" Misty didn't give Cat a chance to respond. "It *is* the new guy. I knew it. He was too good to be true. Is he married? He really does have a girlfriend. I'm going to kill him. Give me his name and I'll take care of him for you. I swear, Cat. I swear."

It had been a mistake calling Misty. Gosh, why had she been so stupid in calling her friend?

Emotions, deep and raw, clutched at her chest and she didn't dare say a word because she would start to cry.

"I'm coming right over. Stay there." Before Cat could protest, her friend had hung up."

Shit!

Cat closed her eyes and let the tears run freely down her cheeks. That's why she'd called her friend. For support, to get her through this nightmare.

Gosh, how could she not have seen it? A guy who wanted his cock tattooed like a tentacle had to be nuts.

Yet, the idea had turned her on. Big-time. Did that mean she was nuts too? Yeah, definitely. To have fallen for a guy who thought he was a shapeshifter. And he thought she was one too! Too freaking funny.

No, she needed to get out of here. She'd reassure Misty that she would be fine and then she'd get the RV packed and be on the road in an hour. Two max.

She would be out of the state and well on her way in a few hours. She could drive all night. She just needed to put distance between herself and Calder.

God! He thought he was a shapeshifter. A freaking what? Part octopus? Like he couldn't have come up with something better than that? Didn't female octopi die after giving birth and the males died after having sex or something?

Catalina slumped onto the kitchen chair and buried her face in her trembling hands. No, she wasn't going anywhere. She was a nervous wreck. She'd get into an accident and get someone killed if she went out like this. She'd really fallen hard for Calder. Fallen hard and fast. Too fast.

But something way in the back of her mind went over what Calder had said about her eyesight getting better and her tattoos looking different. Her skin did look healthier and pinker and—

A knock on her RV door had her jumping out of her chair.

Shit! Customer? She couldn't face a customer now and she seriously couldn't do a job. Her hands were just too shaky. She'd probably end up crying like a blubbering idiot if she opened that door.

Her gut clenched at her next thought.

Maybe Calder had come? There's no way she was going to talk to him again, ever.

"Cat! It's me. Open the door. Are you alright?"

Misty. Thank God. Cat heaved a sigh of relief. On rubbery legs she walked the few steps and opened the door. Misty took one look and shook her head and gathered Cat into a warm embrace, cooing that everything would be all right.

Yeah, this was why she'd called her friend. It was comfort and reassurance she needed. And Catalina let the tears roll freely.

CALDER HAD WANTED TO talk to Cat once again before night fell, but a pristine, white convertible with red interior was parked right beside Catalina's RV and he decided against it. She had company. Probably a client. The last thing he needed was for some witness to see her freaking out when he showed up on her doorstep.

He'd waited as long as he could for her visitor to go, but he had to leave before he shifted. The sun was setting a spectacular spray of gold across the mirrorlike ocean, and had he not been so upset about the terrible way he'd behaved today; he would have enjoyed the sunset.

Instead, he felt dead inside as he motored his houseboat out onto the waters to prepare for the change. Dead, emotionally dead and physically numb.

Maybe, just maybe, he'd lost her forever.

MISTY STAYED WITH CAT for the rest of the day, talking to her, soothing her with red wine and coaxing her to eat a lobster sandwich before stuffing a couple of their favorite comedy DVDs into the player. Cat appreciated Misty's company. Loved her friend dearly for calling in sick for an audition she had in Beverly Hills, but when Misty threatened not to go into work at her waitressing job on the biggest night she made her best tips, Catalina didn't want her friend to suffer financially because of her.

She'd already taken advantage of Misty's friendship, now she needed to draw the line.

Besides, she really wanted to be alone. A loner all her life, she was used to her own company, but somehow tonight there was a really extreme urgency to have no one around.

Giving a reassuring promise to Misty that she wasn't going to leave in the dead of night, at least without saying her goodbyes, her friend reluctantly left to get ready for work.

While cleaning the few dishes, Catalina glanced out the tiny kitchenette window and her breath caught at the beauty in the golden sunset. Long shadows scurried across her yard and the marina a mile down the coast where Calder had his houseboat. Her gut plummeted as his houseboat headed out to the open sea. Despite not wanting to, her heart longed to be with him. Out in the quiet, dark depths of the ocean, making love and simply being.

You are a sick fuck. She could never be with a guy who was as mentally disturbed as he obviously seemed to be. On top of that, he believed she was a shapeshifter too. Even to insinuate her tattoos were altering due to her flesh readying for the change.

Nutjob.

She'd call it a really early night. She would drift off into dreamland and make herself not think of Calder or his tentacles. Locking up, she turned down her air-con a bit and headed for the shower. Undressing, she stepped into the shower and moaned softly at the tender bite as the spray of water pummeled her flesh.

Huh. Odd for her skin to be so sensitive. Almost as is if she'd lain out in the sun for too long and had been mildly burned. But all over? Hadn't Calder said something about sensitive skin? The guy was insane. She needed to stop thinking of the things he'd said.

She hurried cleaning herself and when she was finished, she stepped out of the shower. Reaching for the bath towel from the hanger beside the door, she caught sight of herself in the mirror and couldn't help but be taken aback at the beauty of her tattoos. The tentacles that climbed over both of her shoulders looked so vibrant, as if they were real. Even more real than normal. Even better than last night. They pulsed and shimmered and she gasped in horror as parts of her flesh literally seemed to smooth. Not just her tattoos, but her *flesh*. Just like Calder had said about her skin changing. Cat shook her head as a rush of denial flooded her.

Too much wine. That's the problem. She wrapped the towel around her body and quickly headed for bed. The fact the soles of her feet were incredibly sensitive too as she padded into her bedroom registered quite deeply in her mind. And as she slipped beneath her light, summer sheets, the material almost drove her nuts at the wicked way it caressed her flesh. She tossed aside the sheets, opting to sleep without them. But when the mattress beneath irritated her beyond belief, she wanted a soothing bath.

Unfortunately, she didn't have a bathtub. But the ocean was just steps away. A nice refreshing swim would get her feeling better.

It was already dark outside and, since the camp spot her RV was parked in had tall privacy hedges on both sides of the property and the moon hadn't come up, she was able to pad naked around to the back, unseen by any curious eyes. Taking a look up and down the beach, she groaned in relief to find it empty of people. Most of her neighbors were elderly and quiet and the rest of the people seemed to work nights or were maybe making supper.

Sprinting from the cover of the bushes, she sighed as the fine grains of sand sifted between her toes and the sultry warm breeze whispered against her flesh.

Instincts were leading her now. She'd find the relief she craved in the cold depths of the ocean. Everything else was suddenly forgotten. Her anger toward Calder disintegrated as she slipped quietly into the cool, tranquil water.

Heavenly. Absolutely heavenly.

HER ENTICING SCENT drifted along the currents. It made his three hearts pound insanely hard and, using his tentacles, he stroked through the water and made it to Catalina's side within minutes. He had excellent eyesight, despite it being so dark down here, and could see she'd changed. She lay on the sandy bottom, her legs and arms transformed into tentacles. She blinked beautifully at him with questions in her wonderful blue eyes. But he couldn't explain anything to her while in their Octoposeidon bodies. Yes, they still had their mouths, but speaking under water was kind of hard. He would have to wait until they shifted back again and, even then, she might not remember as temporary amnesia during the first few shifts were a high occurrence until the brain caught up with the body.

At nights they lived on instinct and the need for her sexual release emanated from her in intoxicating waves.

He needed to take her. Now, before any other males caught her scent and showed up to fight for her.

She was timid as he approached. Understandable. She didn't know she'd turned. She was dazed and didn't realize yet he'd spoken the truth today. Or that she'd been human only moments earlier.

As he reached out a tentacle, she tensed, possibly aware of what he wanted to do with her. Aware and ready. Her four limbs flowed toward him in the current. Eagerly he met them. Their suckers aligned perfectly as he latched onto her, suction cups fusing. They matched beautifully.

He moved his body against hers and quickly impaled her, his engorged cock sliding deep into her vagina. He groaned at her tight, hot, moist grip.

Quickly, he released his sperm into her. This would keep predator males away, show them this female was claimed by emitting his scent along with hers into the ocean currents. Only the extremely aggressive males would come now, if they dared. He was a big Octoposeidon, and he would fight to the death for her. If he lost the fight, the other male would lay claim to Catalina by sucking Calder's sperm from her vagina and replacing them with his own.

Over his dead body. She was his and his alone.

They would do this every night for the rest of their lives. Fuck, eat, swim and sleep. In that order. She shuddered beneath him as he plunged a tentacle into her tight ass. Another of his tentacles held her firmly around her waist as he thrust his swollen tentacles in and out of her ass and pussy. She mewled sweetly as she convulsed and climaxed. Then he slid a swollen tentacle into her mouth, silencing her gasps of pleasure as he triple penetrated her. He plunged and thrust until once again she was writhing and convulsing and trembling into another all-consuming orgasm. Perfect, his mind said happily. Absolutely perfect.

Chapter Seven

C atalina awoke smug and comfortable in her small, air-conditioned bedroom. Thankfully whatever had gripped her last night was gone. She felt wonderful, satisfied. Too much wine and not enough food, that's what it must have been. She snuggled her face into her feather pillow. Gosh, she didn't even remember coming out of the ocean after her swim. But her dreams had been filled with lust and sex and leisurely swimming without a care. All of it in a dark, watery world and Calder had been the one fucking her.

Her eyes popped open.

Calder.

Damn him. Why did she have such wonderfully sensual dreams of a crazy man?

"How do you feel?" Calder's voice curled out of the corner of her bedroom, slicing panic into her.

She bolted into a seated position. "Oh my God! What are you doing here? Get out of here!" she yelled at him.

Sweet mercy! He was a serial killer, and she was his next victim. She scrambled out of bed. She didn't know how she did it so quickly nor did she remember doing it, but he caught her around her waist, his hand clapping over her mouth, preventing her from screaming.

He held her firmly against him. And that scared her even more. She struggled against his grip, but he held tight.

"I won't hurt you. I promise."

No! He probably said that to all his victims!

"We need to talk this through," he said softly in her ear. "What you experienced last night wasn't a dream. We were together. When morning came, you and I shifted back into full-human form."

He was insane!

"You'll begin to remember all of this soon. It's just at the beginning when you shift the memory is slow in catching up."

Insane!

"I know this is really hard for you. It's because we're in human form. We've lost the ability to follow our instincts, but when we're in our Octoposeidon form we are at a primal level. Nothing else matters *but* instincts. You seem to have calmed a little. Can I remove my hand now? You won't scream?"

She shook her head. Oh, she'd scream all right and she'd do it the instant she got clear of him.

He un-cupped his hand from her mouth and, to her surprise, he let go of her waist. She didn't waste any time running. She hit the screen door with her hands so hard she didn't realize it was latched until it refused to move.

Finally, with the shakiest hands she'd ever had, she managed to slide the bolt. She screamed as the door flew open, yet at the same time his strong arm curled around her waist like a vise once again.

Her feet left the stairs as he lifted her back into her RV. But she'd noticed they were no longer in the park, surrounded by people. She'd seen only wide-open fields. The bastard had moved the RV! He had taken her to a second location. Hysteria snapped through her. She began to fight harder against his grip, punching his rock-hard arms and kicking his legs.

But he didn't budge. The man was solid muscle, and she was so going to be dead if she didn't get away from him.

"Easy, Catalina. Easy."

"Let me go! I won't tell anyone about this. Just let me go."

Normally she was so strong and in control of her emotions, but now she was terrified.

"It'll be dark soon," he whispered.

"What?" She'd been sleeping all day? He must have drugged her. Again.

"Males normally shift before females. When the sun sets, you'll see me shift. And then you'll believe."

Weariness laced his voice, and she stopped fighting. She was wasting her strength. She would wait him out and escape at her first chance. To her shock, he let go of her and she didn't know how she managed to walk the few steps on her wobbly legs, but she did and practically fell onto her breakfast nook bench.

"You may not shift tonight. When shifting first begins, it's sporadic. I didn't expect you to shift the first night we met, but I sensed you were close because of your scent. And then last night your scent was even stronger so I knew you probably would, and you did."

Her scent?

"It was strong enough to lure me from twenty miles up the coast when you drove by my marina the other day in your RV."

Oh God, he looked so serious. He really believed this bullshit.

"We Octoposeidons tire easily until we've shifted several times. In a couple of weeks, you'll be energetic, and you can carry on your human activities as if nothing really happened. It's important to our sanity to carry on as normal as possible. Especially at the beginning."

She tensed as he sat on the bench across from her. He was naked and acting as if it was perfectly normal for him to be walking around nude. And she was naked too. Surprisingly, she wasn't the least bit embarrassed about him seeing her this way. She was just terrified.

Adrenaline. It had to be the adrenaline that was making her immune to embarrassment.

"Once you see it with your own eyes, you'll be okay. Are you hungry? I picked up some things for us while we were on the road."

"Where are we?"

She'd find her cell phone and dial 9-1-1. That's what she would do.

"Not too far away from your campsite. This land actually belongs to me. It's private. About half a mile up the coast is my marina. I own it. That's the way I earn my living. As shifters we prefer to stay close to the ocean. It's easier that way." He grinned.

She wished she could warm to him, but she couldn't. He was crazy.

"Not hungry?" he asked.

She shook her head. She couldn't eat. How in the hell did he ever expect her to?

"That's okay. You ate quite a lot last night. We had many easy catches. You learn quickly."

He didn't look crazy. He seemed to believe everything he was saying. He really, truly did. *Whack job!*

"Tonight, after you watch me shift, there might be a slight chance you..." He let the words trail off and his shoulders slumped as if in defeat. Emotions, sharp and raw, slammed into her. She didn't want him to experience sadness.

She jolted in surprise. *No, don't empathize with him.* She needed *him* to have empathy for *her.* She's the one who'd been kidnapped.

"Sometimes the human mind cannot fully comprehend what we truly are."

Oh, sweet mercy, she was so going to lose it. Panic began to grip her. She forced herself to remain seated and listen to him. There really wasn't anything else she could do. If she ran, he'd be on her in a second.

"I can give you something to keep you calm." His direct gaze made her uneasy. *What if he really is speaking the truth?* She chased away that rogue thought. Like she could trust him? If she believed his story then, yes, she would be insane.

"Let's move the trailer," she said. "We can head back to my place. The beach there is more familiar to me."

He remained silent. Anxiety gave her the courage to keep talking.

"What if I turn? I won't be in familiar surroundings. I'll be scared."

That's it, Cat. Make him see how much he is scaring you.

Suddenly, unexpectedly, his tense features softened and for a split second she relaxed and thought he was normal. That he was the same guy she'd fallen for.

But he's not.

"I'm sorry. I'm really sorry I'm scaring you. We do have a website with more information on our kind."

She blinked in confusion. *A website?*

"Pretty much every Octoposeidon is a member, and we have private forums and stuff to catch up with each other. Others, loners who prefer not to mate, don't join."

Okay, maybe she could keep him talking about his kind. She could stall until sunset. Until he "disappeared" into the water. Then she could make a break for it?

She glanced out the windows, hoping for signs of a highway somewhere in the near distance. Nothing. Just fields of waving grass and rolling hills to her right, and then to her left, the ocean.

Shit.

"Okay, so what's the URL? Maybe I can surf? Maybe it'll help me out?"

Once she got online, she'd send Misty an email to call the cops.

He sighed heavily. "I think it's best if we head down to the beach now. It's getting dark and the need to change is increasing. Put on your robe if you're more comfortable. It's your human side that may be...ashamed of your attire."

She nodded. Before she could make a move to the bedroom where she remembered leaving the robe, and where she had every intention of locking herself inside, he waved for her to remain seated. Disappointment rocked her.

"I'll get it. It's over there." He nodded to the small, kitchen countertop where her short, terrycloth swim robe had been placed.

"The URL to the site is in the pocket. When I shift, I won't be able to shift back until sunrise. I ask only one thing. That you believe your eyes and give me the benefit of the doubt. I hope you'll visit the site and find as much information as you need."

"Sure, sure." Yeah, right. She was like so out of here when he went into that water.

He got up off the seat, grabbed her robe and held it open for her. Suddenly she became self-conscious as she moved off the seat and his sharp, hungry gaze studied her every movement. She held her breath as she turned her back to him and slipped her arms into the robe sleeves.

"Your tattoos aren't shimmering, so you won't be changing tonight. But if you look at mine..."

Okay, she would have to stare at his cock. It was the only area she'd tattooed. She forced herself to turn back around and look down at his semi-erect shaft.

Her breath halted at the beautiful sight. The tentacle he said she'd tattooed all around his cock was literally shimmering, as if maybe he'd put glitter on himself or something.

"We have to hurry." There was an urgency in his voice as he grabbed her hand, his strong fingers intertwining with hers.

Oh no, she hoped he wasn't going to kill her. Yet instinctively she somehow knew he would never hurt her.

Okay girl, ignore your fucking instincts! Fight and run! She blew out a hard breath and forced herself to follow him down her RV steps and into the warm, salt-tinged air.

It was almost dark and damned if that tentacle tattoo of his wasn't glowing. They stopped at the water's edge.

"Come on in."

She shook her head. "I'm fine here."

"I won't drown you. I promise." His white teeth flashed in the darkness as he chuckled. Well, at least one of them was having fun.

"Just a few steps in. I want you holding my hand when I turn and I need a couple of feet of water so I can breathe."

Fine. To her surprise her instincts were getting stronger. They were urging her to move into the water with him. Stupid girl that she was, she was actually allowing him to pull her in farther.

Suddenly, an exquisite scent drifted through the air. The enticing aroma wrapped around her body and cuddled her, held her, caressed her.

She moaned softly as she leaned closer to him. His body was warm and hard.

He didn't say anything. He just stood beside her, facing the ocean, looking out at the big, white, full moon hanging on the midnight-blue water.

His breathing was growing hoarse and more erratic. Her heart beat faster and her eyes widened as he dropped to his knees. The splash of water sounded like an explosion.

He let go of her hand and she instantly thought about running, but then the intoxicating scent riveted her to stay beside him.

Earlier, he'd mentioned she had a scent. Obviously, he had one too. It was lovely. It made her heart pound faster and made her want to be with him. She stood in stunned fascination as Calder's arms suddenly seemed to soften and grow smaller and rounder and shorter, until they were shaped like tentacles. His head and torso remained in human form.

Okay, she was officially insane.

It happened within thirty seconds. Not more than a moment ago a man had fallen to his knees right in front of her and now Calder's arms had turned to tentacles and a couple more of them peeked out from the water. His legs? Yes, his arms and legs were now tentacles, just like when she'd thought she'd fantasized or dreamed or whatever the hell those things had been when she'd had sex with him in the ocean.

Disbelief rocked her.

"This cannot be happening," she whispered, totally awestruck at what she'd just witnessed. She held her breath as he lifted a tentacle and pushed his ear forward, angling his head so she could see the back of his ear.

Oh, my goodness. Gills?

"I need to dive under as when I am in this shape, I can't breathe air." His voice was croaky, as if he truly was gasping for air.

And then without another word he turned around, slipped beneath the calm ocean water and disappeared, leaving only an array of circles playing along the top of the water.

She didn't know how long she stood there, staring, before she finally remembered how to walk.

Despite his disappearing into the water, his strong scent still wafted around her in waves. He wasn't too far away, and she needed to be here with him. That thought, of course, totally confused her due to the fact he'd kidnapped her.

Instincts. He'd said in this Octoposeidon form she'd live by her instincts. But she hadn't turned tonight, and her instincts were telling her to be near him.

"Oh, come on," she blurted, her voice echoing in the still night air, making her tense with wariness. What if he got hurt out there in the ocean? What if he got killed by predators?

She swallowed at her suddenly dry throat and focused on trying to think of what she should do next. A huge part of her urged her to stay and wait here for him to come back to her. He was her mate. He'd fucked her in the ocean depths. He'd claimed her in order to protect her and because he loved her.

Oh, come on, Cat. You've flipped your freaking lid. He's probably drugged you and you're hallucinating all this.

Another part of her, the curious side, urged her to explore all possibilities that maybe, just maybe, he was telling the truth. Her hand slipped into the pocket of her robe, and she found a piece of paper. Suddenly, she knew what to do.

CALDER LAY AT THE DEPTHS of the sandy ocean floor and waited for the golden rays of sunshine to do its magic and transform him back to human form. It had been a long and lonely night without Catalina. The anguish of thinking she might not be there when he came back out of the water had just about driven him mad. After what seemed like an eternity, the morning finally arrived, and he swam closer to shore. As the sun split over the horizon, its bright rays splashed into the water and Calder felt the stirrings of the approaching change.

Impatience raged through him as his tentacles slowly receded into his body and his human shape began to shift. Blood poured into his limbs and the familiar crushing pressure increased inside him as his body realigned and his bones reformed.

When he could no longer breathe in the water, he popped his head past the surface and sucked fresh, salty air deep into his newly converted lungs. Immediately he opened his eyes and searched the beach. Surprise and excitement crashed through him as he spied Catalina's large RV with its colorful splash of sea life creatures emblazoned on the side.

She hadn't left?

During the long, lonely night, he'd convinced himself she wouldn't be here. As blood poured through his limbs, his strength returned.

Finally, after several moments, he could stand. The sturdy sand beneath his feet allowed him to move swiftly toward the beach and her RV. Although he could travel faster as an Octoposeidon by using his tentacles, he'd learned to move quickly after a change into human form, and he took off at a dead run out of the water.

He made it to the side door of the RV and halted. No sound came from within, and his hearts dropped in despair. Had she walked out of here? Had she gone to the authorities? Were they on their way to arrest him?

A surge of adrenaline pounded through him and with intense wariness he surveyed the surrounding fields for any sign of activity. Nothing moved except the ankle-high grass. About two miles out in the ocean, he spied a sailboat and then a cruiser, but nothing to indicate a problem.

If he was ever caught, he would have to either escape or kill himself with the death pill embedded safely and deeply inside his thigh, before night fell, to avoid exposing his race. Humans hadn't evolved enough in order to be trustworthy with a species such as shapeshifters. Until they were honorable, his kind would continue to protect their species via suicide.

As Calder lifted the latch on the door, he was surprised to find it unlocked. Although if she had run for help, she wouldn't have bothered to lock up anyway.

He padded up the two steps into the interior and immediately found her. Apparently, she'd closed the windows as the trailer was very warm, and her scent intoxicated him to the point where he wanted to wake her and start fucking her. But he held himself under strict control. He didn't want to frighten her again.

His breath backed up in his lungs. She'd fallen asleep, her face cradled in her arms, propped on top of the small table. The laptop sat right in front of her. The website URL and password he'd written on the card and put in her robe pocket lay on the table beside the laptop. Even if the authorities had come and found the card and used it, they would think the site was just for kooks.

Calder grinned down at Catalina. Such a beautiful human with her soft, silky, auburn tresses and smooth skin. He ran his fingertip along her wrist to her elbow and sucked in a hot breath when she whimpered softly. Yes, even in sleep she would know his touch, his scent. He'd been her first Octoposeidon and she would always know him.

He touched the screen on the laptop, and it flared to life, bringing vivid images of the mating section of the Octoposeidon website. Erotic pictures of shifters with their human torsos and tentacle arms and legs intertwined, or swollen tentacles penetrating mouths, vaginas and asses, had his breath coming faster.

He wondered if she believed him now. Wondered if her instincts for preserving their kind ran as deep as his own. The first week of an Octoposeidon's change was always the most vulnerable time for their species. The octopus side was rarely an issue. It was the human side of the shifting that caused most of their problems.

Confusion. Insanity. Denial. Suicide. He hoped Catalina would embrace who she really was.

There would, of course, be many questions. On both sides. The urge to fuck her grew more intense as he continued to inhale her succulent scent. When a female slept and dreamed of sex or when she was close to her mate, her sensual odor was always present. Those were the most dangerous times for the human side of the female Octoposeidon, giving her away to fellow Octos who might be in the area.

Right now, she was giving off an extremely seductive aroma and it was wreaking havoc with his self-control. Perhaps that's why she had kept her windows closed? Because she'd read the warnings on the website?

Excitement pounded through him at that hope.

"Catalina," he whispered. His voice sounded too hoarse. Desperate. He needed to calm himself or he would frighten her. Or then again, if she got him even more aroused, his smell would fire off his skin and seduce *her* into *his* arms.

He needed to wake her before he grew even more heady. They needed to talk.

"Catalina," he repeated, this time a little louder.

She whimpered again, a sexy little moan that had him wanting to hoist her up on the table and slide his tentacle-tattooed shaft deep into the snug warmth of her pussy. He smiled down at her as she blinked. Warmth melted through his entire body as she lifted her head and stared at him. His gut hollowed out at the momentary flash of fear shifting through her pretty, sky-blue eyes.

Then it was gone. Replaced by trust and acceptance. Instincts told him her brain had successfully made the transition. Her human side had caught up with her Octoposeidon side. He hadn't anticipated it to happen this quickly. He'd expected a few more days of holding her here against her will, and then shifting together to Octo form and back to human form before her instincts for self-preservation would kick in. She was smarter than he'd given her credit for.

"Hey," she whispered and smiled. The beauty of it stabbed deep into his hearts like a ray of sunshine, lifting his spirits and increasing his urgency to mate with her.

"You smell nice," she said, tilting her head as she gazed up at him. Her lips were slightly parted, as if she were expecting a kiss. Dare he kiss her?

Shit. His odor was seducing her. Ah, hell. He'd just have to go for it.

CATALINA SHOULD BE afraid of him. At least a part of her brain was telling her that, but her need to be with him was pushing away the remnants of fear with every breath. By studying that website she'd begun to understand the things that had been happening to her. The intense sexual dreams, her crazy attraction to Calder, her fascination with tentacles and why she'd been blacking out.

Okay, so she wasn't pure human. She'd get over it. She had to.

"We need to talk," he whispered as his head drew closer and, to her delight, his lips tingled softly across her mouth, leaving her wanting more. So much more.

"About?"

He pulled away and straightened.

"Us," he said.

She really liked the sound of that.

"You can't tell anyone about what we are, Cat. Pure humans can't handle it." His tone was serious, and she forced herself to focus on being serious too. Kind of hard when all she wanted was the sexy man's tattooed cock buried deep inside her.

"I know. I went through the website with a fine-toothed comb."

"Yeah, I know it's fascinating stuff about discovering there is another species living among the human population, but you can't tell any of your friends. Under any circumstances."

"I understand." After witnessing his transformation, she'd gone online and read everything on that site. Her brain fully comprehended the seriousness of the situation and the dangers of being a female Octoposeidon, especially during the times when males smelled her and might fight Calder to get her.

It was weird how easily she'd accepted what she'd read. How it all made sense.

"I don't understand why my mother and father never told me the truth. How could they not tell me? I remember when my mom was alive, I always had babysitters at night. Mom and Dad worked nights, or so they said. My mom was at home during the day, and she took care of me. My dad worked as a teacher at the local college. I just thought he was a workaholic. I never questioned why he worked so much. And when my mom passed away, the woman he remarried must be an Octoposeidon."

"Once a male has a female and he loses her, he finds it extremely difficult to continue living, so he is forced to find and fight for a mate quickly. Your father was lucky to have found two mates in his lifetime. As you have read on the website, females are rare."

She nodded, remembering reading that.

"They probably didn't tell you because they were trying to protect you. Many times, the child remains human and never changes. Sometimes parents decide to keep their shapeshifting a secret from the child to give them as normal a life as possible. There's no real way to know if a child will change until the scent."

Catalina smiled as warmth splashed through her. "Oh yes, the scent. Which, by the way, I love on you. You smell too good to resist, my man with the tentacle tattoo. Too good to resist."

His eyes flared a deeper shade of green, and he leaned closer. "I love you, Catalina. I've loved you from the moment I first smelled you."

"I can honestly say the same, Calder. I love you too."

"When do I get the rest of my tattoo?" he whispered against her mouth.

"After. We have more important things to do at the moment," she replied.

Excitement laced his face, and his mouth descended upon hers again, his warm lips making love to hers. He made her entire body tingle, and her instincts told her she finally fit in somewhere. It was awesome, this strong sense of belonging. She wouldn't trade it for anything in the world. She was going to love this new way of life, and she was going to love Calder.

Forever.

Bared to Him

Jan Springer
A Tentacles Shape Shifter Erotic Romance
Human by day and a tentacle shape shifter by night, Gray Wagner, is
the *last* male that Alaskan custom boat maker Miranda Bolton dreams
of falling in love with. He's irritating, arrogant and teases her to no
end. Due to her ancestry, Miranda knows she has a good chance at
becoming a shifter just like Gray. Alone with him, traveling the high
seas on a yacht, she unexpectedly can't stop fantasizing about him.
Suddenly Gray becomes the *only* one she wants to mate with, and she's
going to make sure she gets what she wants...

Gray Wagner promised Miranda's dad that he would keep his daughter
safe during their week-long ocean voyage to attend a mutual friend's
wedding in California, but Miranda's succulent scent is driving Gray
wild. He knows he shouldn't be thinking about doing all the dirty and
delicious things he wants to do to her, but all his promises to
Miranda's father disintegrate when Miranda shifts and Gray goes
primal...

Chapter One

Near Sitka, Alaska

M iranda Bolton was brushing waterproof stain onto the last strip of the custom-made cherry trim on the exterior of the yacht's wheelhouse when a nearby noise made her look up. She trembled as she spied her father's partner, sexy as sin Gray Wagner, standing completely naked on the deck right in front of her. He studied her carefully as he held the base of his erection. With his other hand, he leisurely stroked the massive length.

"You're the most gorgeous woman I've ever seen," he whispered.

Disbelief rocked her. For years, he'd been teasing her and keeping her at arm's length, and now suddenly he wanted her. It was a dream come true.

He stalked toward her, his stride confident and determined.

"I want to make love to you, right here and now," he said.

His mid-length dark brown hair ruffled beneath the Alaskan ocean wind. His body heat wrapped around her, making her want to snuggle into him. Her breath caught as he dipped his head, and his lips gently caressed the corner of her quivering mouth.

Gosh, he smelled so good. The combination of fresh soap, a tinge of sea salt, and his primal male scent reminded her of a storm with her helplessly caught right in the middle. His sweet caresses on her mouth turned stronger until he slid his lips fully over hers in a commanding kiss that sent shockwaves right to her very core.

A wonderful headiness zapped through Miranda, tossing her slightly off balance. Instinctively, she reached out and curled her hands over his shoulders in an effort to steady herself. Hot muscles bunched beneath her fingers, making her moan at the unbelievable strength he seemed to possess.

He thrust his tongue past her lips, boldly parted her teeth and dueled with her tongue. Her breathing quickened as incredible sensations seared around her like a sparkling waterfall. Nerve endings she didn't even know existed ignited.

Miranda leaned against him, her curves fusing with his powerful length. She whimpered as his callused hands slid around her waist. He held her tight and pressed his erection against her tender core. Need ignited deep inside her. Suddenly she yearned to have him thrusting inside her.

She pressed her body harder against his. But he pulled away. His eyes were heavy-lidded, his lips slightly parted. His breaths came swift and harsh.

"Not yet," he whispered.

Huh? Not yet? I'm ready. So ready for him.

Her mind spiraled. She needed him. Wanted him. Craved for him to make love to her. To make her *belong* to him.

His hands went to the buttons on her blouse. Within a blink, her top was off, and her breasts bounced free. Miranda cried out in surprise as Gray lowered his head. A sexual rush whipped through her as his heated mouth melted over her left nipple. All thoughts disintegrated as he pulled and twisted her flesh until it throbbed with a wickedly delightful ache. Then he moved to her other breast. His mouth was like a heat-seeking missile as his tongue laved and lashed her tender bud.

When both her nipples were swollen, and aching with pleasure-pain, he let go of her waist and dropped to his knees in front of her.

"These shorts will have to go," he said as he gazed up at her. The wild look in his eyes stoked an inferno deep inside her.

She exhaled slowly as he slid his fingers beneath the waistband of her cotton shorts. He yanked them and her underwear down. Her legs were trembling so much she could barely lift each foot to step out of her clothing. He tossed them aside.

"I've been waiting so long to taste you."

She still couldn't believe this was finally happening, that Gray was interested in her.

Her heart crashed against her chest, and she held her breath as he dipped his face between her thighs. Heat and pleasure blistered over her as he lapped and swirled his tongue around and over her aching clitoris. Her thighs trembled and she moaned as he sucked and nipped at her tender flesh.

He slipped a finger inside her, and her muscles clenched around the sweet intrusion. He withdrew and thrust two fingers into her. She bucked and her thighs tightened. He moved his lips over her clit and suckled.

Pleasure arced through her with lightning speed. Exquisite shudders rocked her. Heat seared down her channel as he sucked her cream from her body.

He thrust his fingers in and out in a frenzy. As she gyrated against him, he kept up the frantic pace. Mind-destroying vibrations tore through her, and she bucked uncontrollably.

"Gray! Oh! Gray!"

How in the world had she ever believed she couldn't stand this man? How had she ever believed she hated him?

"Your dad says we've been invited to a wedding. Where's the invite and who's it from?"

Miranda snapped back to reality as his deep voice slashed her sensual fantasy to smithereens. She gasped for air as she discovered she was still on her hands and knees, the can of waterproofing liquid in front of her, the paintbrush in her hand.

Oh, gosh. The man in her fantasy was standing right behind her. Like, how embarrassing.

Heat flushed her cheeks. She blew out a tense breath and dared not look up from the wood trim she'd been staining. Damn! It had just been a fantasy. But why had the fantasy seemed so real? How could she have gone so deeply into it? So profoundly that she'd felt him touching her and experienced such intense pleasure?

She heard the flutter of paper as he picked up the wedding invitations where she'd placed them on a clipboard on a nearby lounge. She felt his excitement sift through the air as he read it.

Wow, she was so in tune with the man lately, it was scary.

She'd hoped to be long gone before Gray had returned from a business meeting in Oregon. She hadn't wanted to see him. She was still pissed off at him for asserting to her father he should be the one delivering this yacht to California instead of her.

He'd insisted she should be staying here at the secluded Alaskan inlet where it was safe for a young woman. Taunting her with bullshit that the three-thousand-plus-mile trip down the coastline, in a yacht, all by her little self was too dangerous for a female. Well, she'd practically been raised on the ocean, and she'd experienced how unpredictable the weather could be. She also had a couple of guns, and she knew how to shoot if there was any trouble where humans were concerned.

Crap! She wasn't young either. She was twenty-five years old, and she was damned ready to show them both that she was quite capable of taking their custom-made yachts onto the ocean and delivering them on her own. She knew how to run the radar, read the maps and check the marine forecast. She knew where all the quiet, safe inlets were located, and she knew how to operate the radio if there was trouble.

Until Gray had shown up on the scene several years ago, she had gone with her dad on all the runs. There had never been a problem that couldn't be handled, especially with all their connections along the coastline.

Thankfully, her father had agreed with her, and this was going to be her maiden voyage. She was so looking forward to proving to her father, and to Gray, that she was just as reliable as Gray was in delivering a yacht to a customer thousands of miles away.

"You're early. We weren't expecting you until tomorrow night," she said. She was surprised her voice sounded so calm, despite just being caught fantasizing about him.

"Missed me, did you?" His arrogant tone annoyed her. For some insane reason, she didn't want him to know she trembled with excitement every time she smelled his dominant Octoposeidon scent. She didn't want to react to him, but she knew why it was happening. Despite not really wanting to become an Octo, she was oddly calm about it happening. She was going to change, and she may as well just accept it.

Living as an Octoposeidon shapeshifter was a dangerous life. Every twilight, Octo shape shifters had an irresistible urge to get into the ocean. Their arms and legs turned into three- or four-foot-long tentacles, their internal organs re-organized, allowing them to breathe and to survive underwater.

While in the depths of the ocean, they were at the mercy of predators. At dawn, they returned to human form and lived on land. All of this was thanks to the god Poseidon, who'd mated with an octopus. They'd created a new life form and ever since, the Octo had kept their existence a secret from the human world.

Going through the change meant she would want to mate, and the last male on Earth she wanted to mate with was Gray. He was an irritating man, yet his nearness made her want to lose her self-control.

"The invitation is from Calder." Shock was quite evident in Gray's voice. She'd been just as surprised to discover their mutual friend had found a mate because there were so few Octo females around.

"Glad to see he's hooked a female. Wonder where he found her? Maybe I should go and check out the California currents and see if I can fish one out for myself. It's been way too long..." He let the words drift and to her horror, her cheeks heated.

Meaning too long since he'd bedded a female. Despite trying to ignore him, she was so annoyed at what he was saying that she turned and looked up at him.

He looked scruffy-hot wearing tight blue jeans and his black-and-blue-checkered flannel shirt. His dark-brown hair ruffled gently in the breeze. and a sexy five o'clock shadow lined his cheeks and chin. He had that familiar teasing smirk on his face and his gray eyes studied her for a reaction. Well, damn him, he wasn't going to get one.

She turned away. She dipped and withdrew the brush from the can and slapped more of the stain onto the trim.

"What did your dad say about the invitation? Is he letting you go?" he asked in a snarky voice that cracked her restraint.

"I don't need his permission. I am old enough to decide whether I am going to a wedding or not."

Asshole.

"I'm talking about delivering this yacht. Isn't it due to the customer within a week? Can you do both?"

"The wedding is in California. I'll deliver the yacht and then pop in for the ceremony. No biggie. I'll give them your regards while I'm there." She doubted Gray would fly down there for a wedding when business was booming here.

"Do you have a date for the wedding and reception?" His voice had suddenly changed to a lower tone. One with an odd, dissatisfied growl that she'd never heard before from him.

"That's none of your business."

"No, she doesn't have a date." Her dad's loud voice boomed across the yacht as he suddenly appeared on the gangplank.

"Don't you think she needs one?" Gray prodded in that teasing voice again.

She turned and tossed her dad a warning look. She was not in the mood for Gray's stupid teasing this afternoon.

"She has one," her dad replied. He winked at her and she got an overwhelming urge to run to him and hug him. She loved hugging him. He was like a thin version of Santa Claus with his long straggly hair and white beard and mustache.

Thank you, Dad!

"She does? But you just said..."

Her dad held up his hand to silence Gray.

"Our customer for this yacht just called. He's decided on some changes. He wants that large forward cabin made into two cabins, and he wants the extra bathroom built beside the existing one, so each cabin will get its own bathroom. He is willing to pay the extra costs of some of Gray's exclusive carpentry designs, plus there is a good-sized bonus in it for the both of you if the delivery date remains the same. Remember, the yacht is for his wife's surprise birthday party."

Miranda frowned.

"But Gray can't put up the walls and install everything before I leave tonight."

A serious no-argument look splashed across his face, and she got the feeling she wasn't going to like what her dad was about to say.

"I've already ordered the necessary supplies and reworked the itinerary. Supplies will be ready at various ports. That'll give Gray the time he needs before you reach California."

Her gut hollowed out in frustration. Damn! She'd been looking forward to doing her first solo run and proving to them that she was as good as they were. Hell, she was even better than they were.

"Oh, so you've decided to let Gray take the boat instead of me." She didn't like being pulled off a job promised to her, and she found it hard to keep the disappointment out of her voice.

Her father smiled and his blue eyes twinkled with unmistakable mischief.

"Gray will be going with you, Miranda. He can't steer and do the job and sleep."

"Both of us?" To her surprise, Gray echoed the same words at the same time as she did.

Her dad's bushy white eyebrows furrowed.

"If either of you has a problem with that, you will need to set it aside. The bonus will allow us to get that second building you two are always harping on. Lord knows having you two working in separate buildings will keep the arguments down to a dull roar."

Her dad studied her, as if expecting an argument. Well, he wasn't going to get one, at least not in front of Gray.

"You both set sail tonight. Gray, come on to my office and I'll give you the lowdown on the trip. Follow the new changes to the schedule I just created and there won't be any problems."

Her dad turned to her.

"And, Miranda, since Gray is going with you, and you'll need a bodyguard to fend off any human males and Octoposeidon males, you'll have a date for the wedding. It will be Gray."

She heard Gray curse softly beneath his breath. She didn't have to look at him to know the idea sucked as much for him as it did for her.

She was about to mount an argument with her dad, when his cell phone rang. He dug it out of his shirt pocket and looked at the screen. He smiled.

"Looks like your business meeting paid off, Gray. Our next customer is calling. I have to get this."

"But Dad..."

He held up his hand to silence her. "Now don't argue with me, sweet pea. I don't have the time."

He began speaking to his customer as he headed toward the gangplank.

"You should look happy, Randi." Gray said her nickname so softly it felt like velvet smoothing over her senses. "You won't have to show up solo for that wedding. See you later."

Gray winked at her and the smug expression on his face had her cursing him under her breath. He tossed her an amused smile that made her want to throw the paintbrush at his broad back. With a wave of his hand and an overly satisfied stride in his walk, he followed her dad down the gangplank.

"YOU MAY AS WELL FACE it, Jack. She's going to turn. I've noticed some changes to that effect," Gray said as he poured himself a coffee in Jack's office and gazed out the nearby window to watch Miranda. She stood at the bow of the bright white sixty-foot yacht they would deliver to California.

She was gazing at the giant puffs of storm clouds looming off the western horizon. The way the sun hit them, made the clouds appear almost black. Watching her silhouetted against nature, her long sandy-brown hair billowing behind her in the October ocean breeze, made his breath catch. He wanted her so badly. But he couldn't make a move on her and claim her as his female because of his loyalty to Jack. Jack had made it clear on several occasions that he hoped Miranda would remain human and get a nice human man to take care of her.

He knew he should sugarcoat it so that Jack would have some time to get used to the idea that Miranda wasn't going to remain a pure human, but he couldn't. Returning today from that business meeting and finding Miranda on the boat, her sensual scent practically bringing

Gray to his knees with want for her, had alerted him she would soon change.

Jack nodded. Devastation was evident on the sixty-two-year-old man's wrinkled face. Perhaps her father had also noticed the subtle changes in her recently. Her skin was glowing a vibrant, healthy pink. She was hanging out on the ocean more often, finding all kinds of excuses to take motorboat rides across the waves. There was that restlessness in her that made her want to go and deliver that yacht on her own. The truth was that deep down inside her, an instinct was telling her she needed to get away and find a mate.

"It's another reason why I want you to accompany her, Gray. You'll keep the males away from her. You'll keep her safe. I know I can trust you."

Guilt shifted through Gray like sharp razorblades. He knew he should tell Jack he wasn't sure he could handle staying away from Miranda. Her scent drove him wild. Lately, every time he saw her, he wanted to take her into his arms and kiss her. He craved to touch her in ways a guy in charge of her safety should not be thinking about. And, at nights when he turned in the depths of the ocean, he swam alone in the darkness, needing her. *Wanting her.*

Jack's slap to his back snapped Gray from his thoughts.

"She'll be safe with you. You don't know how good that makes me feel."

Yeah, right.

Gray forced himself to smile at his partner and then took a sip of the scorching hot coffee. He grimaced as the fiery liquid slid down his throat. Perfect. Just the way he liked it. But the heat of the coffee did nothing to douse the chaos of his emotions. Guilt ruled. How was *he* going to protect Miranda from himself?

"Have you unpacked from your other trip yet?" Jack asked as he handed Gray the new itinerary.

Gray shook his head and pocketed the schedule. He'd look at it later and then give it to Miranda.

"No, but I need a fresh set of clothes. I can pack in a few short minutes. Then I just need to add a suit for the wedding. I can order a rental over the Internet and have it waiting for me in California."

Jack nodded.

"Good. Good. Seriously, I am glad I hired you all those years ago. I knew you would be the perfect man to protect her if she went into the change. Do you think she has an idea she won't be the human she's always wanted to be?"

She knows.

But he didn't tell Jack that or the fact he'd been reacting to her. Jack was human. He didn't have to know everything about Octo males and how badly they hungered for a female.

"I think you'd have to ask her that question," Gray said.

Jack frowned. He gazed out the eastern window of the office and rubbed a hand across his scrubby white beard. Gorgeous snow-capped mountains loomed behind the handful of colorful buildings nestled amongst the cliffs of this secluded hamlet. It was a beautiful place here and it almost made Gray's breath catch at how close he'd come to never coming here in the first place.

"I've been her mother, her father, friend, and confidant since her mother died. She's always wanted to remain human, like me."

You mean you taught her to want to be human. But Gray kept the comment to himself. He'd never agreed with the way Jack catered to Miranda's sporadic comments of wanting to remain a human. The chances were pretty much for sure that soon, at every twilight, her legs and arms would shift into octopus form. Her craving for sex in both her human form and her Octo shape would become a dominant part of her life. Just as it was for Gray.

"I'll have a talk with her when you both return," Jack replied softly.

Gray was sure Jack's talk would come too late. Again, he remained silent. Jack would find out soon enough.

"In the meantime, I should let you know we got the job from that business tycoon you were meeting with. He's slapping down three million for a sailing yacht and wants it ready for spring. That will be Miranda's run."

Gray nodded, barely hearing Jack's words as the older man continued chatting about the new job.

He was so damned glad he'd returned earlier from his trip. Had she gone to that wedding alone, she would have been prey to strange Octoposeidon, and Gray didn't want her first Octo sexual experiences with one or more strangers. He wanted her first time to be with *him*.

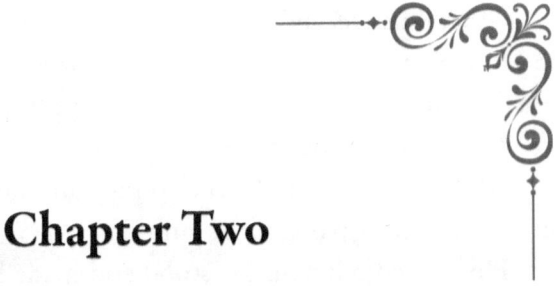

Chapter Two

The instant Gray left her dad's office and strolled up the outside stairs to where the three of them shared a large apartment on the second floor of their office building, Miranda left the yacht. A few minutes later, she knocked on her dad's office door. Without waiting for him to call out for her to enter, she walked in.

"Dad, we need to talk."

"Hey, sweet pea. Are you all packed up for your trip?" he asked.

He didn't look up as he studied some papers on his desk. She could tell in the way he worried his bottom lip that he didn't want to deal with her now. She almost dropped the argument she had planned, but decided she owed it to herself to stick up for herself.

"I just have to get my stuff on board. Dad, you promised I could do a solo run this year. It's already October and unusually mild this year. Perfect boating weather. I had my heart set on going this one alone." Guilt did wonders on her dad when she wanted something, and she wasn't above using it on occasion. Like now.

He looked up and surprise washed over his face.

"You know why you can't go it alone this time, Miranda," he said and returned to studying his papers.

"I get that. But I want a promise from you that the next one is mine."

He frowned and looked up at her again. He shook his head.

"That'll be December. The ocean is not a good place for you to be in December, sweet pea. Gray is experienced with the winter deliveries. He'll do the December run. You can do next spring."

Gray. Gray. Gray. Damn him!

"Promise me, Dad. All the spring runs are mine." May as well get more than one trip out of the guilt.

He seemed relieved. He stood and made his way around his desk and engulfed her in a warm embrace that was more like a tight bear hug.

"My baby is growing up," he whispered against her ear.

His baby. Gosh, was he for real? She'd stopped being a baby years ago.

"I'm impressed you didn't argue more about this run. You're turning into a real professional. I promise. Spring runs will be yours," he said as he let her go. He gazed at her with love in his eyes and it made *her* feel guilty for extracting this promise out of him.

"You be very careful out there, sweet pea. Keep an eye on the marine forecast. Storms can sneak up on you this time of the year."

"I will."

"And don't argue with Gray when you're out there. You two need each other to keep this delivery on time. You can run the boat nights while Gray takes to the ocean and follows you. In the mornings, you can both sleep. He'll do the renovations to the yacht in the afternoons and evenings. Gray has the itinerary. Stick with it and you'll have no problems."

Miranda nodded. She could promise to stick with the schedule, but Gray, on the other hand, was going to be a problem. Especially with that earlier sexual fantasy still very fresh in her mind and affecting her body.

AS MIRANDA HAULED HER belongings below deck to the master cabin, she thought about her past. For her entire life, she'd craved being near the ocean. That urge had really come out following the tragic death of her mother. She'd been five and her dad had moved the two of them inland. But Miranda had grown depressed and moody, crying and begging to go back home. Home, meaning the ocean.

Therefore, in his overprotectiveness, he'd then moved them here to the secluded bay near the Alaskan Glacier Park. Here, with the stunning backdrop of snow-capped mountains and glistening ocean waves and an abundance of nature, Jack had built his custom-made yacht business and homeschooled Miranda. In turn, she had flourished.

Miranda smiled at the memories of carefree days as she followed moose and deer in the nearby woods, taking the motorboat out and chasing the seagulls. The air was fresh and salt-tinged, and the evening sunsets were spectacular. This evening was no exception, she thought, as she climbed topside and took her place at the helm.

Ahead of her, the horizon glowed gold. Behind her, her dad stood on the dock and waved goodbye. She returned his wave and then reluctantly turned away as a bubble of emotions snapped through her. Quickly she brushed away some renegade tears, took a deep breath, and put the yacht into a faster pace.

She truly loved her dad, but it seriously was time to break free of his tight restraints on all aspects of her life. She looked out at the moody ocean.

Somewhere out there, Gray was already swimming beneath the dark waters, doing God knew what. Until recently, she hadn't been interested in his nocturnal turnings. However, tonight there was an invisible pull to gaze out into the darkness and search for a sign of him. But she saw nothing except the full moon slowly lifting out of the ocean horizon and an occasional glitter of silver rings as a fish jumped out of the water and splashed back in.

Giving up her search for Gray, she steered the yacht out of the bay. Tonight, the water was choppy, and the October breeze was cold. She didn't waste any time closing the nearby windows. In order to make good time, they would do as her dad instructed. She would pilot the boat during the nights, and they would sleep during the mornings when the yacht was anchored. Gray would work on what needed doing through the afternoons. It was best if she stayed away from him, because he both irritated and fascinated her at the same time.

Man, she just wished she wasn't so damned confused about him.

LONELINESS WRAPPED around Gray as he swam through the murky ocean water. He used the currents to help him move along with the yacht. He munched on whatever seafood got in his way, and he kept his hearing tuned to the sound of the yacht's motor nearby.

When the need to see her could hold him back no longer, he popped his head above the surface and sniffed the air, inhaling Miranda's succulent scent. Every time he smelled her, his cock swelled. Along with it, came an intense need to lure her into the water with him. He wanted to swim with her, mate with her, and just have her with him all the time.

Life as an Octoposeidon wasn't easy. He spent his nights napping, eating, and steering clear of predators and craving female companionship. But females were scarce. They were the weaker of the species and many died at birth. It did not matter if she was born as a human during the day or born as an Octoposeidon during by night. No one knew why most females didn't survive. It just was.

The sudden urge to get back under the water to breathe grabbed him and reluctantly he followed his need for survival.

BRITISH COLUMBIA, NORTH Coast

It was just after dawn when Gray turned back into his human form. He was soaking wet and naked as he climbed up the yacht ladder and padded across the deck. Miranda had been motoring for more than twelve hours, with him propelling himself along behind her. He'd had no trouble keeping up with the fast pace, and she'd dropped anchor over an hour ago. Since then, he'd been waiting in the chilly waters to return to his human form so he could get back onto the boat.

He knew he should try to get some sleep. However, resting was the last thing he wanted, especially with Miranda on board. The instant he'd climbed out of the water, her sensual scent had captured his full attention. As he let himself into the wheelhouse, he gazed down at himself.

An extreme tightness had grabbed his balls. His penis was at full mast. It was engorged and aching like a son of a bitch. Frustration burned through him as he opened the windows and allowed the fresh air to blow away her scent.

He knew he should not let her smell get into the air. It would carry for miles in the wind and capture the attention of any other Octoposeidon males in the area. But, this morning, he just had to find a way to get her off his mind, and getting rid of her scent was hopefully going to help. Besides, by the time any Octo male caught wind of her, they'd be long gone from this area.

He was about to press the button to pull up anchor when a sexy little sound drifted through the wheelhouse. He paused. Miranda? Was she masturbating? Sure, he'd heard her moaning away in her bedroom back in the building he shared with her and her father. He'd listened at her bedroom door plenty of times while she'd pleasured herself.

It was a good thing her father was hard of hearing and had his bedroom far away from the area where he and Miranda slept, or Jack would have put a stop to Gray sneaking around outside Miranda's bedroom, the way he'd been doing the past few months.

"Just pull up anchor and turn on the engines and get the hell moving, Gray," he muttered to himself. The engines would drown out her sexy mews and he could get on with the day. Yet, he hesitated.

A soft gasp drifted to his ears. His cock hardened some more. He swallowed.

Don't go down there. Gray. Stay here.

Even as he was warning himself, he was moving out of the wheelhouse, heading down the stairwell and stepping into the narrow companionway that led to Miranda's cabin. Her scent was powerful down here and it took everything in his being to stay away from her.

A soft cry. A gasp. A broken moan.

He stayed at the doorway and listened. Excitement pounded him. Need tore through him.

She cried out again. He reached out and his fingers rested on the knob. He wavered.

What the hell are you doing? Jack put you in charge of her safety. You owe it to him to keep her safe. Even from you.

A muffled wail shot through the companionway. His resolve broke. He opened her door.

Her sweet, intoxicating fragrance crushed his self-restraint, and he stepped into the cabin. Early morning light streamed in through the several portholes, illuminating her.

She was lying on her side in the king-sized bed. Blankets had tangled around her body. Her cute feet stuck out from beneath the sheets, but he had no problem making out her curves pressing against the covers. Her hair looked like a golden waterfall splayed out on the pillow. Long, black eyelashes framed her closed eyes, and a hint of blush had swept across her cheeks.

She looked like an angel. So beautiful. So perfect.

His.

He swallowed and took a few more steps into the room. Her breathing was fast, and she moaned softly again. The sound clutched at him. He slipped both his hands in front of his thighs and grabbed his cock. It jerked hot and wild as he stroked himself. His flesh strained and burned against his fingers, the veins pulsing against his palms.

She cried out again and he suddenly realized she wasn't masturbating. She was fucking dreaming.

Irritation snapped through him. Who the fuck was she fantasizing about? He knew that females experienced extreme sexual fantasies shortly before they went into the change. It happened while they were awake and while they slept. It appeared she was having one now. Her wickedly attractive aroma certainly attested to that fact.

"Gray?" she whispered.

She was fantasizing about him. Why would she be dreaming about him after all the teasing he'd done to keep her away from him?

She moved off her side and onto her back. She thrust her arms out. The blankets drifted off her neck and down, revealing her breasts.

Oh, man. This was so not good. But really good at the same time. He bit his lower lip and stifled a groan as he studied her. Her breasts weren't large nor were they small. They were just right, and he knew they would fit perfectly into his palms. Her areoles were big, and round and her nipples were huge and erect.

She cried out his name again.

His gut twisted. Sexual hunger tore through him. His cock throbbed. He winced.

Her feminine aroma made him dizzy with need.

He needed relief. Big time. He had to get out of here before the last shred of his self-control tore away and he climbed on top of her and made love to her.

He could barely walk as he slipped out of her room. Up in the wheelhouse, he pulled up anchor and started the engine. Thankfully, the rumble drowned her sexy sounds, but her scent continued to cloak him and taunt him.

Defeat made him curse. He reached down and wrapped his fingers around his erection. With his other hand, he stroked the growing length. Instantly, pleasure spiraled along his shaft. He squeezed his eyes shut and let his breath escape between his lips.

With a steady rhythm, he rubbed himself harder and faster. His body tightened. Sensations, hot and sharp, snapped along his length. His thoughts and his restraint disintegrated. He thrust his cockhead against a nearby computer console, gasping at the cool hardness of the smooth plastic.

Pleasure exploded into shudders and poured through him. His legs weakened. He cried out Miranda's name as he came.

HAVE MERCY! MIRANDA moaned as she awoke to arousal coursing through her and the cracking of her heart beating way too loudly in her ears.

Oh wait. It wasn't her heart. Someone *was* hammering. It took her a few seconds to orient herself as a foreign room rolled into view. Then she remembered. She wasn't making love with Gray as she'd been dreaming, but she was sleeping on the yacht.

She'd been unusually tired and wickedly aroused all last night, and before turning in to sleep she'd left a note for Gray, telling him not to worry about making noise. That extra wall and everything that came with it, plus the new bathroom, had to be finished, and she needed to get away from him as soon as possible. These sex dreams she was having about him were breaking down her resistance.

Miranda's vagina convulsed just thinking of him. She could smell him too. Sweat, soft-scented soap and prime male. She inhaled deeply and allowed his smell to invade all her senses. She trembled as images of Gray erupted inside her mind again.

Visions of his muscular arms wrapping around her waist and holding her steady. Of her looking down and watching his thick, pulsing shaft slide inside her.

Oh! This was getting utterly ridiculous. Why couldn't she stop thinking about him?

Maybe you should fuck him, a naughty voice prodded from somewhere in the back of her mind.

Shut up! Shut up!

She needed to get out of bed and into the shower. A cold shower. Then she'd figure out what to do next.

GRAY ADMIRED THE PARTIALLY completed bathroom he'd been working on all afternoon. While Miranda had been in the throes of her sleep fantasies, he'd pulled up anchor and motored along the coast in record time. The fuel tanks had been refilled with diesel at Prince Rupert, and he'd picked up supplies at the other ports Jack had indicated on the itinerary.

Late morning, he'd anchored in a secluded bay along the southern coast of British Columbia. He'd had a quick bite to eat and then set to work. Since he was a carpenter, certified electrician and a plumber, he'd been able to work quickly and efficiently on parts of all the rooms.

He'd tried to remain as quiet as possible, knowing Miranda would need her rest so she could take over the helm during the night, but the compressor, the drill and circular saw made such a racket.

After having had no sleep himself, he felt surprisingly wide-awake. Hell, he wouldn't have been able to sleep if he'd tried. That orgasm he'd experienced early this morning had blown his freaking mind. He thought he'd be relieved afterward, but he was still aroused to the point it was damned irritating.

As he'd worked, he noticed her sexy Octo scent was getting stronger with each passing hour. It continued to create havoc on his senses, to the point where he'd worked like a maniac and sweat had poured off him. Unfortunately, work did not put much of a damper on his need to mate with her.

Late afternoon had come quickly and when he went to the engine room to get more of the supplies, he heard Miranda's shower running.

Shit! She was up and soaping her beautiful human curves. He ached to climb into the shower with her and caress her soft-looking skin. Craved to kiss her pouty mouth and catch her gasps as he thrust into her wet heat.

Oh man! He needed to get off this yacht and away from her, or he was going to lose his self-control and start making love to her!

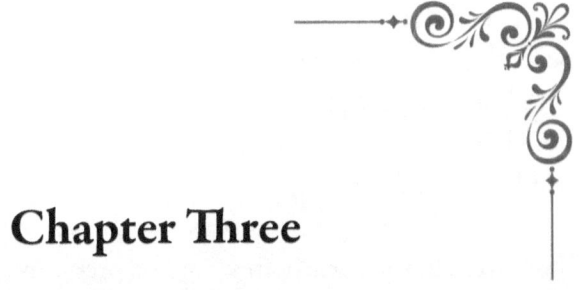

Chapter Three

After her shower, Miranda used every excuse under the sun to stay in her cabin. She'd eaten some fruit that she'd placed in her cabin's tiny refrigerator, dressed, stared out the port windows at the mist-shrouded ocean, and now, after sitting around on the bed for a couple of hours working on some puzzles in a game magazine she'd brought along, she was starving again. She realized too that it was excessively quiet. Actually, Gray had been silent since she'd stepped out of the shower.

Where had he gotten off to?

She tiptoed to her cabin door and opened it. She listened. Not a sound. For someone with a deadline, he didn't seem to be in a hurry to finish.

She took a deep breath, grabbed her courage, and stepped into the hallway. Curiosity urged her to check out how much he'd gotten done while she'd slept. If he was in there laying tiles or doing whatever, then she'd praise his work and get the hell away from him.

But as she walked down the companionway, past the engine room and along the forward companionway, she didn't smell his fresh unique smell. He'd been here, but the scent was dissipating.

A moment later, she stood in the new bathroom that separated the two new rooms. Surprise made her gasp. How in the word had he managed to do so much work in such a short time? It appeared as if the bathroom was almost finished. It looked spectacular and followed the same gray and white theme of the rest of the yacht's interior.

The toilet was in, and a pristine white marble floor gleamed beneath the lights. He'd placed the black and gray marble counter with the dark gray drawers and double gold sinks. He'd even done the cherrywood trim along the ceiling and accents around the port windows and doors.

The only thing missing was the shower stall and a mirror. Once those were in the bathroom would be pretty much done.

She peeked into the two new cabins. Both of them looked identical. Pristine white padded walls, and Gray's elegant cherrywood trim. The two double beds that had been in the original forward cabin, had been separated. One double bed occupied each of the rooms. The only other items needed were some custom-made cabinets that Gray would build and a couple more pieces of furniture, which they would pick up somewhere in Oregon.

But where was Gray? A sudden unexplained sense of urgency swept over her. Had something happened to him? It wasn't time for him to change. Twilight was at least a couple of hours away. So where could a man go on a yacht? Unless he'd taken the emergency dinghy to shore and something had happened to him?

The sense of insistence snapped into one of alarm and she quickly left the cabin. She rushed along the narrow companionway to the engine room. He wasn't there. She checked the salon, but he wasn't there. No sign of him on deck either. The dinghy hadn't been used. So where was he?

Golden rays of late-afternoon sunshine tore through the mist and splashed down upon the yacht. She turned and surveyed the coastline. The fog that had been prevalent all day was dissipating and she suddenly realized they weren't at the same inlet where she'd anchored. He must have moved them while she'd slept.

"Gray!" she shouted, hoping her voice would carry on the brisk wind.

No answer.

"Gray! Where the hell are you?" she called out again as she stepped to the bow.

"Wow! You sleep like the dead," Gray called up to her.

Miranda tensed and quickly looked over the railing. Gray was swimming in the ocean right below her. And he was nude!

Tanned muscles bunched everywhere on his body, and she meant everywhere...across his chest, his arms and his belly and waist and...

She shivered when she spied his giant erection shimmering beneath the clear water.

"Do you like what you see?" he asked. His voice was soft and alluring as he gazed up at her.

For a split second, she wanted to tear off her clothes and jump into the water with him. But his cocky grin shot through the magnetic pull.

"You don't have anything I haven't already seen on a human male," she teased.

For a brief moment, anger blazed in his gray eyes. It excited her that he might actually be jealous that she'd had sex with a human male, although she hadn't.

Then, just as quickly, his look turned to something else...heat, passion, need for sex. Need for her?

Her breath halted as he swam around to the forward port side of the yacht. His big hands grabbed the gleaming silver rails of the ladder, and he slowly rose out of the ocean. Silvery beads of water clung to his body, and she couldn't stop herself from staring at him and lowering her gaze to...

Wow! Out of the water, his shaft appeared even bigger! He was so well hung! She'd never seen a guy built like him. Not even in those naughty magazines that her dad kept hidden in a locked desk drawer in his office. She'd found the key one day to that drawer, and she'd been transfixed by the occasional naked man in the pictures having sex with the women. But none of those men had a penis *this* size.

She hadn't even realized he was standing right in front of her now, until he spoke.

"You'd better get out of here before I do something that we both know I shouldn't do."

He stood mere inches from her now. She could feel his body heat caressing her skin. Sweet tingles made her inner muscles clench as she remembered how intense his shaft had felt penetrating her during her fantasies. She could smell the salt-scented water clinging to his flesh, and she ached to lick it off *all* parts of him.

She didn't move. Couldn't, even if she'd wanted to. And she didn't want to.

"Randi..." His voice sounded tortured, desperate.

She couldn't say a word as she continued to stare at his cock.

It was perfection. Ultra long. Scrumptiously thick. And so angry and powerful looking. Much better than any fantasy she could ever dream up. She trembled as his hot palms slipped against her hands. His fingers intertwined with hers. He held her so tenderly she'd no idea a man could touch her as if she were something precious and fragile.

He leaned closer and his breath feathered some strands of loose hair off her cheeks. She could feel the tension in his body. Sensed the need for sex rising from him.

"Miranda.". His voice was stronger this time. Commanding. She forced herself to rip her gaze from his succulent shaft and followed the thin dark arrow of hair that wandered over all those delightful wet abdominal muscles to where it sprayed lightly over his chest.

His nipples looked beaded and erect, and his neck was corded with tension. A sexy, dark shadowy bristle caressed his chin. A muscle popped in his left cheek, and then she finally looked into his eyes.

Intense desire sparkled there. Her breath stalled. Her need for him to touch her and to fuck her almost overwhelmed her. If she could have spoken, she would have demanded he make love to her. But she couldn't utter a word because his face was drawing closer to hers.

She closed her eyes, and her heart picked up a maddening pace. His sweet, hot lips melted over hers in such a caressing kiss that senses she never even knew existed flared to life. Instincts told her he wanted to mate with her. That he'd wanted to for some time.

The pressure of his kiss grew fiercer, dominating. He ground his hot erection against her lower belly, and even though she wore a couple of layers of clothing, the tight knot of his arousal branded her flesh.

He broke the kiss, and his breath splashed heat against her face.

"Miranda..." he whispered hoarsely.

Slowly he drew her hands downward until she touched his thick shaft. Then he let her go, and his hands settled on each side of her face and his mouth fused over hers again. His kiss rocketed sweet sensations through her, and she shuddered at the intensity.

She wrapped her hands around his rod and felt it jerk against her palms. He groaned and kissed her harder. Her thoughts spiraled.

She kissed him back. Her lips melted against his until he opened his mouth and thrust his tongue into her mouth. Her senses rocked. This was much better than her fantasies about him.

His cock jerked again. She squeezed his hard penis and began eagerly exploring the silky texture. Her fingers trailed over the pulsing elevated veins until she reached the mushroom shaped cockhead. He groaned again, tearing his mouth from hers.

Her lips tingled from the wicked kiss, and she opened her eyes to find a wild look flaring across his face. His gray eyes were so dark they were almost black. She'd never seen him looking like this before. It both frightened and exhilarated her.

"I want you on your knees, Miranda," he breathed. "On your knees so I can show you exactly how you should be fantasizing about me while you're sleeping."

She jolted at his words. How did he know she'd been fantasizing?

He didn't wait for her to do as he commanded. Instead, he gently, but forcefully pushed her down onto her knees in front of him. When she let go of his penis, it bobbed mere inches from her mouth. Pre-come glistened from the slit of his bulging cockhead.

"Suck me, Miranda. I've waited for too damned long. I need to have your sweet lips wrapped around me."

Fear and excitement gripped her, and she trembled at the husky darkness in his voice.

"Come on, baby. Open that sweet mouth of yours," he ordered.

His penis jerked as he reached down and wrapped his hand about halfway up his shaft. Then he moved closer to her face.

She whimpered as he pushed against her lips. She'd never done this before, but suddenly she wanted to do it. She parted her lips. Gray groaned and swore softly.

She trembled as he slid his flesh into her mouth. Her lips stretched as he pushed further until his hard flesh touched the back of her tonsils and pulsed against her cheeks.

Sweet Octoposeidon! Having him in her mouth felt so...erotic. She moved her tongue beneath his steel-hard shaft. He moaned and his flesh shuddered. She tasted pre-come. He withdrew and then plunged into her mouth again.

"Suck it," he ordered harshly.

Her lips tightened tentatively around his flesh. He groaned sexily and his shaft pulsed in her mouth. She hollowed out her cheeks and sucked. Hard.

He cursed softly and withdrew.

"Put your hands where mine are," he grumbled in a deep, thick voice.

She looked up at him. His face was flushed. His eyes were wild and desperate.

She reached up and placed her hands where his had just been. She wrapped her fingers around his hot thickness. To her surprise, he thrust his fingers through her hair. He held tight to some strands until sparks of pleasure-pain ripped across her scalp.

His breathing grew faster and rougher. He slid back into her mouth, and she slurped on his pulsing flesh. She tasted more pre-come. She liked the taste.

Gray began a slow thrust. Miranda struggled to keep up, caressing his hot flesh with her tongue and using her teeth to feel the power as he slid in and out. His thrusts grew faster, and she bobbed her head, accepting him. His fingers tightened even more in her hair, and she winced at the pleasure-pain. But she liked the way he pulled her hair. It felt good.

He gasped harshly as he pistoned his hips against her and plunged his flesh in and out of her mouth. Faster and faster. She loved how his flesh filled her mouth. Enjoyed the heat, the strength, and the stinging way his searing flesh bruised her lips.

He moaned and called out her name. Her vagina clenched at the desperate hoarseness echoing around her. His penis tensed and tightened. It jerked and thickened even more. He thrust harder. Once, twice, three times.

Thick jets of semen pulsed into her mouth, and she quickly swallowed. She sucked harder and drew more from his shaft. Instinctively, she grabbed his scrotum and kneaded his balls. He groaned and his body quivered as he shot another load into her mouth.

When she could draw no more semen, he withdrew.

She blinked up at him as he looked down at her with a glassy-eyed look. His chest heaved with his every breath.

"I need to get more work done before I turn," he whispered.

She nodded numbly as disappointment rocked her.

His eyes spoke of a need to fuck her. She wanted to tell him to take her right here. Right now. But he'd already left.

She blew out a tense breath and licked her tingling lips.

Damn, she had no idea Gray could make her lose her control so quickly. She really *had* to stay far away from him. However, even as she thought it, she knew she was lying to herself. She needed to feel his penis not only pulsing inside her mouth again but pounding into her too.

She realized it was only a matter of time before both of them fully lost control.

GRAY MANAGED TO AVOID her for the rest of the evening and finally slipped into the cool waters to await the change.

What had happened earlier on the deck with Miranda's mouth wrapped so intensely around his shaft and then what had almost happened after that...

Shit! His cock had been on fire and already at half-mast ready to take her. His legs had been shaky and weak when he had walked away from her. It had taken every single ounce of his strength to turn his back on the look of disappointment on her face, when all he'd wanted to do was to take her into his arms. He'd wanted to kiss those sweet lips forever and thrust deep into her and claim her as *his*.

It had been too close for comfort. Guilt made him feel terrible. Miranda's father would be devastated if Gray betrayed his trust and mated with her. The last thing he wanted to do was hurt Jack. The human had given him a job and a place to stay after most of the male members of Gray's consortium had been wiped out, and most of the females kidnapped by a renegade group of Octoposeidon.

Ten years ago. Gray had been eighteen in human years at the time of the attack. He'd almost died had it not been for three of his surviving sisters and a brother. They'd been swimming far away from the consortium that night and when they'd returned to their home in Maine, they'd found Gray washed up on the shoreline of their secluded property, a bullet in his back. His sisters had cared for him until he'd been well. His brother, unfortunately, had gone off looking for the missing females.

Gray had never seen or heard from him again. For all he knew, his brother was dead. His three Octoposeidon sisters, however, had decided to live quietly among the humans and pretend they were humans. They had split up, taking residences in secluded areas along the coastlines of the United States.

Both his parents had died in the attack. Due to Jack's late wife being from their consortium and Jack being one of the very few humans trusted by the Octo, Gray had gone to Jack looking for a job. The older man had taken him in, given him a partnership in his boat building business, and taught him everything he knew.

Gray owed him big time. The last thing he should be doing was to be lusting after his daughter the way he'd been doing.

But a primal part of Gray craved to mate with Miranda. With every passing day, that craving grew stronger. He knew he would need to make a gut-wrenching decision. Claim Miranda or totally walk away from the two people who'd become his family.

He grit his teeth as his arms and legs began to throb with the need to turn. He kept his head above water and swam slowly around the yacht. The air was thickening. It was getting harder to breathe. He felt the area behind his ears begin to prickle as they slowly transformed into the apparatus that would allow him to breathe under water.

In seconds, his legs turned into tentacles. His arms quickly followed. His swimming quickened and his breathing became labored. He turned and took one more look at the yacht. It bobbed in the waters, its white hull bright against the backdrop of the full moon. He hoped Miranda would step out onto the deck so he could catch a glimpse of her. She didn't. He cursed softly and a horrible loneliness clutched at his heart and sank deep into his very soul.

He slipped beneath the water.

FROM THE DARKNESS OF the wheelhouse, Miranda watched Gray's head disappear beneath the wavy ocean surface. An odd loneliness speared into her heart. She ached for him. For the first time in her life, she prayed to turn so she could jump into the water and be with Gray.

And for the first time in her life, she actually doubted her sanity. Why was she lusting after an Octo male, who until recently had irritated the crap out of her? Was it merely lust flowing through her body? Or was it something more?

She pushed the button and listened as the chain rattled, and the anchor lifted. A few minutes later, she pushed the ignition. The state-of-the-art engine rumbled to life. As she angled the yacht toward open sea, she quickly closed all the windows, ensuring that her fragrance didn't give away her location to other Octoposeidon males who might want to claim her.

She knew all about the dangers of being a female Octo.

When she'd turned eighteen in human years, their friend Calder had dropped by for a visit. He'd slipped her a piece of paper. On it, he'd written a top-secret domain with a password that would get her into the Octoposeidon website.

He'd told her to check it out for just in case she turned. And he'd made her promise that she would memorize both the name and the password and then destroy the paper and never reveal the existence of the website to anyone, not even her father. She had kept her promise.

Upon visiting the website, she'd been stunned to discover that male and female Octos could stay human all the way into their thirties before they changed, while others changed right at birth. The average for the change was in the mid-twenties.

Dangers lurked for Octoposeidons. One of dangers was how far a female's fragrance could carry in the air and in the water. The smell was strongest before a female's first change and then every night and every morning when she changed forms. The rest of the time, her scent was not as strong.

She knew that because of the intense way she was reacting to Gray; she was now putting both of them in danger. Fear for his safety made her pray he would be safe tonight. Suddenly, she couldn't wait until morning. Couldn't wait until she saw him again and knew he was safe.

Her hands tightened on the helm.

And then what?

She worried her bottom lip and shook her head as she studied the rippling waters ahead. She hoped an answer would come to her by then.

OVER THE NEXT TWO DAYS and two nights, Gray and Miranda made great time continuing along the coastline off British Columbia, past the state of Washington and into Oregon's waters. They managed to avoid each other like the plague. In a small town near the Oregon-Washington border, Gray picked up the required furniture. He'd added the extra cabinets and worked as quietly as possible while putting the shower stall into the new bathroom. Miranda stayed in her cabin until he turned at night.

She was changing. She realized her senses were heightened. At night, when Gray was in the ocean, she could even smell his raw odour whenever he neared the yacht. It was an eerie discovery and pretty cool too. It was as if she had radar where he was concerned.

Sometimes, she thought she could even see him swimming in the dark waters. His tentacles stretched out in front of him, as he swiftly propelled himself along the currents to keep up to the yacht.

Her need to have sex with him was driving her crazy. It had reached the point to where she was masturbating several times during what should have been her sleep time. She was surprised Gray hadn't smelled her, broken down her cabin door, and fucked her properly. The bastard had left her aroused and disappointed after she'd orally made love to him on the deck, and she wanted him more now than ever.

She glanced at the clock and noted dawn would be approaching in a little over an hour. She was tired after hours of operating the yacht. Tired of trying to fight the visions of Gray, naked and lusting for her.

Just thinking of him had her breath backing up in her lungs and her body heating up with fire. A touch of claustrophobia suddenly struck her. An intense need to get out of the wheelhouse and catch some fresh air overwhelmed her. She shut off the engine, angled the yacht into the wind, and let it drift along the stiff breeze.

Outside, she stood at the bow railing and gazed out over the dark ocean. It was mild and cloudy, and there had been no moon through the night. Whirls of white mist danced off the choppy water and she caught Gray's odour. She inhaled it deeply into her lungs and loved the way her body reacted. Tremors coursed through her, her sex clenched and need overwhelmed her.

Suddenly she didn't care if Gray was out there watching her. That thought turned her on. Somehow, he had discovered that she was fantasizing about him. He'd said it shortly before she'd taken him in her mouth. Obviously, that knowledge had aroused him.

She kicked off her running shoes and socks and slipped off her flannel shirt and T-shirt. She tossed both onto the deck. The warm breeze and the cool mist gently caressed her breasts. It felt nice. Reaching up, she ran her hands over her mounds. They felt smooth and swollen beneath her touch.

Her nipples hardened as she tweaked and pinched them. Pleasure-pain zipped through them as she pulled. Her breaths quickened and she could no longer ignore the instant throbbing deep inside her. She needed relief. Now.

She dropped her hands from her breasts, slipped her fingers beneath the waistband of her track pants and panties and then removed both, allowing them to puddle on the deck.

She was nude. Totally and completely naked as she stood at the bow of the yacht. Being in her birthday suit out here on the ocean was a freedom she'd never experienced before, and she enjoyed it.

Stepping forward, she bent over at her waist and rubbed her breasts against the cool railing. The pressure of the smooth metal was just what she needed to keep her nipples stimulated. She caught another whiff of Gray's sensual scent. It was powerful and intoxicating.

Instinctively she knew he was out there watching her. She could *feel* his eyes studying her. Could *feel* his need for her zipping through the misty air.

Heat rushed through her. She creamed warmly, sensing that he craved her as much as she desired him.

Spreading her feet, she then slipped a hand between her thighs. Pleasure coursed through her the instant she touched the swollen bud of her clitoris. She slipped a couple of fingers between her slick labia folds, dipping past the wet entrance and into her hot vagina. She withdrew, and using the cream drenching her fingers as lubricant, she massaged up and down and around her clit.

She moaned softly and breathed harshly as she rubbed harder against the railing. Using her free hand, she plumped first one breast and then the other, increasing the friction. She rocked her hips and plunged her fingers deep into the tight satiny confines of her vagina. She withdrew her fingers and then kneaded them over her clit again.

Quickly, she fell into a sensual, fast rhythm. She closed her eyes and stroked herself, rough and fast, gasping as her body tightened and moaning as arousal pooled hot in her belly. Sensual vibrations came out of nowhere and she jolted as trembling waves of arousal washed over her. She cried out Gray's name and imagined him here, claiming her fully.

She spun out of control, bucked her hips, and melted into the pleasure. A deep hunger for Gray draped over her and as her climax subsided, Miranda moaned her distress. She wanted Gray more now than ever.

Damn! The next time she saw him; she was going to grab him by his shoulders and demand he make love to her! She was finished being mad at him. *She wanted him.* The realization made her laugh and cry at the same time. It was amazing. She wanted Gray.

She jolted as white lightning forked out of the sky not more than a mile ahead of her. Her sexual need disintegrated as an unexplainable instinct for survival collided over her. A storm had crept up on her. Not good.

"Oh crap!" she muttered and began slipping on her clothes. She'd made it a habit to listen to the daily weather reports on the marine station. Today, she'd missed it. She'd have to head toward shore and secure the boat.

A gust of wind blasted against her, almost toppling her over. She steadied herself and quickly finished dressing. Raindrops began spattering against her and the deck. The rain was cold and made her shiver. She grabbed her socks and shoes and slipped them on while she rushed about, battening down the hatches. Then she scampered into the wheelhouse.

Wind rattled the windows, making her tense. When the yacht rocked under an exceptionally large swell, she fell onto a padded bench seat. She gasped as another wave crashed against the bow and a magnificent white waterfall slashed into the window right in front of her. The boat dramatically swayed. She struggled to get to the wheel.

Lightning flashed and thunder rocketed overhead. Goosebumps sailed over her flesh. She swallowed a scream. She couldn't panic. She needed to keep calm.

She grabbed tight to the wheel and angled the boat into the wind.

Anxiety snapped through her like a live wire and her heart picked up a tremendous speed. The yacht jarred again, and the wheel jerked so hard against her hands, she almost lost her grip.

Shit! She'd always thought she was pretty strong, but maybe she'd been wrong. She could barely steer the boat.

A wall of gray water rushed up and pounded against the windows. She lost sight of the coastline and quickly popped on the radar and compass. Despite knowing where land was, she found it impossible to steer the boat closer to shore so she could drop anchor. A creepy feeling of foreboding snapped in around her. A dark emotion clutched at her heart.

Would she ever see Gray again? Was this how her life would end? *Oh, Gray*! *Help me*!

Chapter Four

G ray could smell Miranda's fear slice through the lashing wind the instant his head broke the ocean surface a few hundred yards from the yacht. Huge swells raised him up and then down. The dawn sky was dark gray, and sheets of silvery rain made it difficult to see the boat. Because he could now easily breathe the air, he knew he only had seconds left to propel himself with his tentacles.

Alarm for Miranda's safety made him get to his destination in record time. Seconds later, he was fully back to human form and scrambling up the aft ladder. Forceful waves pummelled him, and he struggled to climb onto the deck.

He was nude, compliments of the turn, and the deck was slippery beneath his bare feet as he ran toward the wheelhouse. Waves lashed over the bow and slammed into him, making him fall several times. At the wheelhouse, he cursed when he discovered the door locked. Through the rain-drenched windows, he made out Miranda's silhouette behind the wheel. By the grimace on her face, he could tell she was struggling to keep the boat from tipping.

He smacked his fists on the window, hoping she could hear above the roar of the wind. He was contemplating heading forward to get into her view, when she spotted him. Relief splashed over her features.

It was at that second; he made his decision. She *would* be his life-mate, no matter what. She was so beautiful in her defiance at not allowing the storm to take the yacht. She was a true sea warrior.

A moment later, she opened the door.

"I couldn't get to the shore," she gasped. She looked tired and scared, totally opposite of how beautiful she'd looked while she'd masturbated on the bow earlier. He'd stayed above water for as long as possible, but his need for oxygen had forced him back under.

"You did good. Real good. Go, have a seat. I'll take over," he commanded.

When she hesitated, he grabbed her hand, tugged her to a lounge seat, and forced her to sit. He buckled the seat belt snugly over her hips and rushed to the wheel.

"Enjoy the ride!" he shouted as he took the helm. He hoped his upbeat voice would inject some courage into her, but she merely smiled weakly.

Immediately he got to work. About an hour later, he'd safely tucked the yacht in a sheltered inlet.

FOR THE FIRST TIME in hours, Miranda allowed herself to relax. They were both safe and it seemed as if the storm had eased, although as she stared out the window toward the west, huge dark gray clouds continued to roll, and lightning flashed.

As Gray sat down on the bench seat beside her, she shook her head and held out her hands to show him they were trembling.

"Thank, God, you came when you did because I was just about to give up..."

He placed his finger on her lips, silencing her.

"The boat is secure. We shouldn't have any more problems." His voice sounded so confident that it sent a calming vibe straight through her.

Up until a few minutes ago, she'd been too terrified to think of anything but survival. She'd barely noted he was naked. Now that they were safe, his dominating scent captured her full attention.

"Are you okay?" he asked.

Concern riveted his face, and he grabbed her hands. His grip was strong and hot, and she welcomed how sweetly he squeezed her fingers with reassurance.

She nodded.

"I think so."

"We're safe. Repeat after me. We are safe."

She giggled. "We are safe."

"Come on, let's get you to bed. You look tired," he whispered.

He pulled her easily to her feet. She seriously thought he would let her go. He had, after all, been avoiding her and she'd been avoiding him and...

"I was watching you...earlier...on the deck."

His eyes darkened with desire as he gazed at her. Heat fused her face. Her instincts had been correct. He *had* been watching her.

"And I liked what I saw, Miranda. If I had been able to, I would have pulled you right into the water with me, and fucked you like I know we both want."

She trembled at the lust thickening his voice.

"But we both know I shouldn't..." he whispered.

Disappointment rocked her. She sensed he was about to let go of her hands, but Miranda stopped him by leaning against him. She inhaled sharply as his hard muscle heat pressed in around her breasts and belly and everywhere his body touched.

The solid knot of his erection pushed boldly against her abdomen, and she moaned at the hot spiral of sensations pooling deep inside her.

Oh, no. There was no way she was going to let him go this time.

"I want you," she whispered.

Amazement lit up his face. Before he could verbally respond and tell her any number of reasons why they shouldn't make love, she moved her head closer and kissed him. His body jerked and an erotic groan tore from somewhere deep in his chest. The guttural sound sent a frenzy of sensual shivers shooting through her.

She raised her hands and cupped the back of his neck. She kissed him harder. He responded quickly, his lips sliding tenderly over hers. Sweet tingling sensations snapped through her. Need uncoiled deep inside of her.

His kiss turned demanding. Her body tightened as pleasure, sharp and tight, arced through her. His unique scent poured off him in dark, tantalizing waves, wrapping around her like a net, capturing her.

Suddenly her feet left the ground as he lifted her into his arms.

Oh my! Hard muscles pressed against her body and his eyes looked so dark, it made her breath back up.

"I'm going to show you what a real fantasy should be like," he whispered as he strolled across the deck. He carried her down the stairs and along the companionway into her room. She thought he would toss her onto her bed and start fucking her as she craved; instead, he brought her into her bathroom and gently placed her on her feet.

"Get naked and get the shower running," he whispered in a hoarse voice. "I'll be back in a minute."

She blinked as he quickly left. For a split second, she wondered if maybe she was having another one of her wicked sexual fantasies. Then she noted the towel she'd used to dry herself from her last shower was still strewn on the floor exactly where she'd left it, after she'd forgotten to pick it up.

Somewhere in the yacht, she heard a door close. Gray. What was he up to? Why had he left? Had his leaving just been an excuse because he'd had second thoughts? But he'd told her to get naked and here she was stalling.

She moaned softly as she removed her clothing, realizing that her skin felt ultra-sensitive pretty much all over her. She was naked now, and she'd just turned on the shower water to a nice toasty temperature when she sensed Gray had come into the room.

His sexy, salty scent drowned her in arousal and scattered all her thoughts away. As she turned to face him, her breath caught as she noticed he held some condom packages in his hands. Ookay, this was definitely not a fantasy dream.

He nodded to the shower.

"Get in," he instructed.

His heated gaze had her moving swiftly into the shower. The steaming water cascaded over her face and shoulders and the rest of her, pummelling her sensitive flesh. She felt his body heat wrapping around her as he stepped into the large stall behind her.

"Turn around and face me," he said. As she did, the water from the shower jets massaged the tight shoulder muscles she'd gotten from gripping the steering wheel. She noted he'd placed the condom packages on a nearby soap dish, within easy reach.

"I have been wanting this forever, Miranda. I've been craving you, watching you, smelling your sexy fragrance."

He fell silent as he grabbed a bar of soap and began soaping her right shoulder. His touch was tender as he rubbed her flesh, paying particular attention to an especially tender muscle. A moment later, he soaped her other shoulder.

"I bet your arms are sore from fighting that storm."

"I'm sore from needing you. Inside me," she replied. No use in being coy. She wanted him and she was going to get him.

He grinned. It was a sexy grin that made her heart burst with something she could only call as happy love.

"I've been sore for months, baby. Listening to you pleasure yourself in your bedroom at night caused a lot of cold showers for me."

Oh my. He'd known she was masturbating. Now, *that* was embarrassing.

Leisurely, as if he had all the time in the world, he ran the bar of soap over and around, and under her left breast. Then he came toward her nipple. He lathered soap over it and then teased her nipple by plumping and tweaking it until pleasure-pain exploded and she was gasping. Then he moved to her other breast, doing the same.

"Listening to your sexy little whimpers while you slept and hearing you call out my name was too much for me to take the other morning. And your scent when you are aroused..."

She followed his gaze as he looked down. She blew out a tense breath upon discovering his erection was an angry red. The thick length was angling up toward his belly. She'd forgotten how huge his shaft could get. Her lips tingled as she remembered how his penis had stretched her mouth and pulsed against her tongue when she'd orally taken him.

She inhaled as he rubbed the bar of soap over her belly and then her abdomen. The water that sluiced over her shoulders allowed him to lather the soap into a slippery lube-like substance. He massaged his hands down her body in circular motions. Having his fingers smoothing over her skin was both electrifying and exciting.

As his soapy hands neared her pubic bone, she swallowed and tensed with excitement. Erotic shivers shuddered through her as he slipped the slippery bar between her thighs and slowly and tenderly rubbed her intimate flesh with it. He lathered around her labia and smoothed it over her clit. A couple of his soapy fingers dipped into her vagina. Intimately, he pressed against her vaginal muscles and before she could experience too much arousal, he dipped his fingers out of her again.

Then he ordered her to turn around to face the shower. The spray splashed over her breasts and her nipples immediately went hard and erect.

She moaned and relaxed her shoulders as he soaped her back, her hips and then inward to her lower back. He lathered her butt cheeks, caressing them intimately with his palms, and then moved to the back of her thighs and the rest of her legs. She was ordered to move forward until the water chased away all of the soap from her body.

A delicious strawberry scent drifted along the wisps of steam as he squirted some of her shampoo into her hair. The scent reminded her of the sweet berries her dad grew out on a small plot of cleared land behind the huge workshop where they created their luxury yachts.

Using his fingers, Gray massaged her scalp with sweet little circles. He took his time, and she moaned softly as her entire body relaxed. Having him touch her was heaven. He made her forget the fear she'd experienced while she'd been fighting the storm. He chased away the terror that had rocked into her that the boat would capsize and she'd drown and never see him again. Those negative thoughts simply disappeared.

When he was finished shampooing her hair, he grabbed the showerhead off its base and aimed the pulsing spray over her hair, rinsing the shampoo. She turned around and he sprayed any remaining soap and shampoo off her.

"You were pretty tense before. Feel better?" he asked as he placed the showerhead back into its base.

She nodded and smiled. Yeah, she was feeling very good.

"Good, and now the fun begins," he said in a throaty voice.

He slid open the shower door, seized a towel from the shelf just outside the stall, and then shut the door. He rolled the towel and then dropped it on the ceramic floor in front of her. The towel was immediately soaked.

What in the world was he up to?

His steel-muscled chest flexed as he grabbed the bar of soap again, and lathered it between his hands, and then he replaced the bar on the soap dish. He dropped onto his haunches directly in front of her, using the towel as support for his knees. His hot breath caressed her. As he looked up at her, his eyes blazed with lust.

Oh. Now she understood.

"Pass me the showerhead."

She did as he asked and handed it to him. He aimed the item at the floor and adjusted it until the spray turned into a pounding jet of water.

Her breaths grew quicker as she realized what he was about to do to her.

"Touch your breasts."

Arousal coursed through her at his rough voice. She did as he asked, the thought of him watching her touching herself almost making her come on the spot.

She kept eye contact with him as she reached up and cupped her breasts. A muscle jumped in his right cheek as he watched. She pulled and twisted her nipples, and they became quite stiff. Tension built quickly inside her.

He slid the showerhead between her thighs. He held the item a few inches away from her body and aimed the pummelling spurts of water at her. She gasped at the intoxicating impact. Using the stream of water, he leisurely traced her labia, spraying the pulsating water over her sleek folds.

With his other hand, he reached up and opened her labia. When the water hit her clit, pleasure zipped through the sensitive bundle of nerves. She cried out at the wicked impact and gyrated her hips as arousal coursed through her.

Quickly, he dropped the showerhead and moved his head forward. She cried out as his ultra-hot mouth melted over her sex. He sucked her clit between his lips, his tongue dabbing and stroking until she shivered at the electric sizzles enveloping her.

Frantic now, she grabbed his head, her fingers twining into his hair. She panted and held tight, bucking against him as she exploded in a shower of pleasure.

His tongue slipped inside her, and he sucked. The exquisite pressure destroyed her senses sending all thoughts to spinning away. Warm cream streamed into his mouth.

She heard him growl as he lapped and sipped at her labia. Her thighs quivered and her legs weakened as he continued to suck. When her tremors ebbed, he grabbed the showerhead and aimed it once against her too-sensitive clit. She shattered as another orgasm quickly mounted.

Before she could come, he dropped the showerhead and gripped her wrists. Forcefully, he pulled her hands from his hair. Her eyes popped open with surprise, but excitement roared through her as he suddenly stood. Using his teeth, he ripped open the condom package and within seconds, he was sheathed.

He turned toward her. His lips were red, his face flushed. His gaze captured hers.

"I want you so bad, Miranda," he whispered. He was breathing harshly, and his voice was so thick with excitement that she could feel his emotions crash over her senses.

Exhilaration. Arousal. Domination.

She whimpered as he lowered his head. His mouth covered hers like a heat-seeking missile. He was immense.

He stopped himself from entering any farther, and then he broke the kiss.

"Do you want me?" he muttered. His hot breath fanned over her face.

Frustration and arousal scrambled through her.

"I want you. I need you. Fuck me," she demanded.

His mouth slid over hers again, his tongue probing deep into her mouth, the invasion sending shivery sensations cascading through her.

He bucked his hips, and she cried out as he thrust into her. Her inner muscles quickly stretched and accommodated the long, swollen intrusion. He withdrew and thrust into her again. The way he angled his cock, his thickness erotically rubbed against her clit, creating an awesome friction. He thrust harder. Faster.

An explosion rocketed through her. She shuddered and gyrated her hips, moving swiftly into the pleasure. Her vagina tightened around his flesh like a vise.

He groaned.

She bucked against him. She loved the quakes raining down on her. Loved the exhilaration dancing through her mind. She loved *him*.

At that thought happiness seared through her. She loved him. Had for some time. Why hadn't she seen it before? She pushed her question away and flowed all the way into the pleasure.

"HOW DOES IT FEEL WHEN you turn?" Miranda asked as she lay wrapped in his strong arms, her vagina pleasantly sore from his powerful thrusts and her emotions so calm and carefree that her laid-back attitude, almost frightened her.

Yet, his scent calmed her right back down. If calm was the right word. As she smelled him, her nostrils flared, and her channel clenched. It seemed as if she could sense every emotion in him now. As if she was in tune with him. It was weird. But she liked it.

"For everyone it's different. Some Turn fast. Some slow. Some have hot fantasies like you do and for others their skin gets ultra-sensitive. There are any number of combinations. All kinds of feelings and emotions during the change." he whispered against her left ear.

Oh, her skin was more than sensitive. She was well on her way to the Change.

"No, I mean *you*. How do you feel just before you turn at twilight?"

He grinned and held her closer. He seemed pleased that she was asking these questions. But she was curious. She wasn't terribly afraid of changing because over the years she'd secretly learned to accept that she might end up like her mother despite her father not wanting her to.

"Well, let me see. When it starts to get dark, there is this incredible pull for me to get into the ocean. So, I follow my instincts, and I get into the water. That's what will happen to you. You'll be scared the first few times it happens but once you get used to it, you'll be fine. My advice is to follow your instincts and you'll be okay."

"How does it feel? Is it painful when your arms and legs turn into tentacles?"

He shook his head.

"Not really. Not for me. Some Octos experience some form of pain. Some don't. I just make sure I'm in the water because it soothes my body. Soon there's tugging and pulling sensations on my limbs. My arms and legs begin to feel longer and plumper as the tentacles form. They begin to feel ultra-sensitive, especially the suction cups and the tips.

"What about...your...cock. What happens? It stays the same, right?" She'd read on the top secret Octoposeidon website that a male's penis remained pretty much the same when they turned. Except for some males, their shafts got bigger. And for females, their vaginas remained intact except a storage area formed during each turn. The area allowed sperm to incubate until she decided to impregnate herself. But while having sex in her human form, she could get pregnant just like a human. During that shift, she had no control over pregnancy, except of course through some form of birth control such as condoms.

"My cock stays intact and acts the same as when I am human. It torments me whenever I think of you."

She was glad she tormented him. It meant he must crave her, just as she was doing him.

"My insides feel different, too, as organs start to readjust themselves. You do know that while in Octo form, we develop three hearts?"

She nodded. "Yes, two hearts pump water through what are similar to gills where they extract oxygen and then the other heart pumps it around the body. Calder told me once that some Octo, including himself, when they revert back to human form, their three hearts remain, while for others they have one, just like a human. That's another reason to make sure Octoposeidons remain a secret from the human population," she said.

"Good girl, you've done your homework. I'm impressed."

"And I know that a breathing apparatus forms behind our ears. Kind of like gills. That's how we can survive beneath the water."

"That's right. We also have a hard time breathing air while we are about to Turn. It's best to stay above the surface for as long as possible so your gills are fully formed before you slip under the water. Some have been known to panic and dive under too quickly and end up drowning."

"Oh, not good."

He smiled. "But good to know."

"What else should I know?"

"Well, while I'm swimming under the sea and I'm all alone at night, I dream about all the delicious things I want to do with you."

She grinned and happiness bubbled through her.

"You dream about me?"

"Yep, just like you do about me. Except mine are while I'm awake and I must say they torture me."

To her surprise, he drew her earlobe into his hot mouth and sucked gently. Incredible sensations whipped through her.

"You sure know your stuff," she giggled.

It was unbelievable at how wonderful he could make her feel.

"I can smell that you're about to turn and I want you to promise me that you'll stay calm when it happens and just follow your instincts. They won't steer you wrong."

Yeah, right.

"When do you think it will happen?" she asked.

He shook his head.

"I don't know. Could be tonight. Could be in a week or two. In almost all cases, the female changes before the male so I can be there to help. In the meantime, we'll just have to take it as it comes."

"Easy for you to say."

He chuckled.

"It will be easy once you get used to how easily your body changes."

"Promise?"

"I promise."

She snuggled closer to him. It felt so right being here in his arms. Like she was safe, protected, and loved.

"And I want you to be my mate," he said.

A thrilling emotion bubbled through her. He wanted her as his *mate*.

"I don't know how your father is going to take it, so I will have to run it by him."

She stiffened. *Run it by her father*? A burst of irritation made her frown.

"You don't have to tell him anything. I'm freaking twenty-five human years old. It's my business who I mate with and who fucks me."

"You don't want him to know about us?" he asked. Surprise was quite evident in his voice.

"Of course, I do. But I'll do the telling when I feel it is appropriate."

"I feel I should tell him. I owe him not to go behind his back."

Miranda turned in his arms and gazed up at him. His jaw was set and his eyes flashed with a seriousness she'd not seen before. She realized he was determined to continue treating her like a child.

"I am a woman, Gray. I don't need my dad's permission, and I'd prefer if you don't tell him anything about us. He's my dad and it's my personal business. Oh Octoposeidon! Why are you trying to embarrass me where he is concerned?"

Anger burst in his eyes.

"Why can't you be mature about this?" he snapped.

Bastard! He was right back to his annoying self again!

"You fuck me, and you call me immature?"

"If the shoe fits..." he said tightly. The muscles in his chest were coiled tightly now and he appeared as tense as she was feeling.

How rude!

Miranda struggled out of his arms and climbed out of bed.

"Well! If you aren't the most insufferable son of a bitch I have ever met!" She began gathering her clothes as he cursed softly.

"I cannot believe this. I just can't," she mumbled as she headed toward the door.

"I should have known better, Miranda. I shouldn't have touched you."

She whirled around and caught him sitting up in bed. He seriously looked regretful. Before he'd fucked her, he *had* said he would regret bedding her, hadn't he.

"No! You shouldn't have fucked me if you thought I wasn't mature enough."

She didn't wait for an answer. She was too pissed off. Seriously, was he not man or Octo enough to say he wanted her to be his mate without going to her father for his approval? Was it too much to ask that he tell her he craved her like crazy? That he wanted her no matter what and he didn't care if her father approved or what her father thought? And he was calling *her* immature?

The man was so irritating that suddenly she had no idea why she was attracted to him. Well, no more. Once they delivered the yacht, they were taking separate flights home. End of story.

DAMN IRRITATING WOMAN, Gray thought as he pulled anchor, switched on the engine and steered the yacht toward the open sea. The storm had subsided, and golden rays of sunshine were peeking through white puffy clouds. The sunlight streamed down and sparked like jewels off the white-capped waves.

The scenery was picture-perfect. He should call Miranda to come and check out the beauty of the sight. He knew she loved afternoons like this, but the last thing he wanted was another argument. He was right about going to Jack and letting him know his intentions toward his daughter. He was right.

End of story.

Chapter Five

Miranda frowned as she watched Gray's head disappear beneath the dark ocean waves. Despite being mad at him, she ached for him too. They hadn't spoken since their argument yesterday. In a couple of days, they would deliver the yacht and then they would go to Calder's marina, where the wedding and reception were taking place. After the wedding, they would head back to their old lives in Alaska.

Suddenly, traveling separately back home just didn't have the appeal it had yesterday. Being mad at him didn't sit well, either. Gosh, before having sex with him, she'd had no problem staying mad at him. Now, she just wanted to be near him.

An overwhelming urge to jump into the ocean suddenly swept over her and almost toppled her. Instincts told her she had only minutes to get into the water in order to survive. Confusion and a wave of dizziness made her grip the wheel. She gazed down at her hands and gasped.

They were pulsating and getting darker. What the hell? Gray had said females turned before males...usually. Oh damn. She would have to be the exception.

Steady, Miranda. Steady.

Was she going to turn? Now? She couldn't turn. The boat wasn't even secure.

Shit. This could not be happening.

Panic zipped through her as the urge to jump into the water grew. She was too far offshore to drop anchor. If she simply left the boat, it would float along unattended. Someone might find it and claim it. Or the Coast Guard would seize it and ask questions.

Maybe she could steer the yacht closer. Maybe...

Hurriedly, she aimed the boat toward the sandy shoreline and jammed the thrusters into full speed. The yacht lurched forward, and she almost lost her footing.

To her horror, she was finding it hard to breathe. Panic snapped through her.

She tried to remember what she'd read on that secret Octoposeidon website and what Calder had said. Some females changed fast. Some slow.

Oh, she hoped she was a slow turner. She just needed a few minutes to get the boat into shallower waters. Her body began to ache in a curious way. Her arms and legs began an odd pulsing and tingling. She needed to swim. She needed to breathe.

When she could no longer stand the incredible need to jump into the ocean, she switched off the engine and dropped anchor. It would drag and catch on something. Hopefully.

She didn't care about the boat anymore. She needed to survive. She could barely get aft; her legs were so wobbly. She stepped onto the transom and dove in. As she impacted the water, the cool liquid sliced like sharp knives against every square inch of her flesh.

Panic screamed through her as her brain warned her that going under water would cause her to drown. But an instinctual drive buried deeper inside her shouted at her to do it. She followed her instincts and slipped her head and body beneath the surface.

GRAY KNEW IMMEDIATELY that something was wrong. Miranda wouldn't have headed the yacht toward shore unless there was a problem. He just hoped to hell that other Octo males hadn't scented her.

Damn! He'd been living in a freaking cocoon where Miranda was concerned. He hadn't taken the dangers seriously. He'd been too passive with her safety. He would have to rectify that situation.

It had taken most of his strength to jet-propel himself through the water with his tentacles to keep up with the yacht. When he saw the anchor slide through the ocean and saw her dive into the waters a few hundred yards in front of him, he knew what was happening.

She was going through the change, and he was witnessing it. Through the clear, dark water, he made out her silhouette as she slowly tread water just beneath the surface. She appeared to be in a daze, not sure of what to do. Her arms and legs had turned into tentacles. Disbelief etched her wide-open eyes as she stared at him.

He wished he could communicate verbally with her and tell her she was going to be all right, but down here under the sea, verbal communication just was not possible.

Instead, he swam closer to her. She was nude. Her clothing had ripped away as her tentacles had formed. Her tentacles looked beautiful. They were dark gray, three feet long, as thick as her arms, tapering off at the ends. Her suction cups glowed an intriguing midnight-blue color, and her sexy scent was playing havoc with his senses. His instincts to mate with her were quickly overtaking his concern for her emotions.

Tentatively, he reached out a tentacle and curled it around her waist. She was warm and luscious against his suction cups. Thankfully, she didn't protest as he drew her against his body. She continued to blink at him, as is she were stunned, but he would have her feeling good in no time.

Holding her steady, he slid two tentacles up along her inner thighs, stopping short of her bare pussy, before running his tentacles back down her legs again.

She shuddered.

Oh, yes. She was very responsive. In Octo form, her human guard and need for self-control would no longer matter. Instincts would take over just as they were doing now. He tensed with appreciation as she twirled the narrow tip of one of her newly formed tentacles around the base of his shaft. The miniature suction cups molded with his flesh. She held him tight and gently squeezed. Her touch sent erotic shivers racing through him.

Gray moaned, and bubbles sifted out of his mouth and rocketed to the surface. He grinned. It appeared as if they were going to make a magnificent coupling.

MIRANDA STARED AT GRAY in disbelief. She was under the ocean surface, in the water and she was having no trouble breathing, just as Gray had said. It was amazing. Her eyesight was magnificent, despite the darkness. A school of rockfish leisurely swam past them. She could smell them, and her mouth watered. She'd catch a meal later.

Gray looked spectacular. His body and head were the same, yet his arms and legs were smooth, long black tentacles of at least four feet each. His suction cups glowed a pretty fluorescent green that she found quite attractive.

Right now, she wanted Gray more than anything she'd ever wanted in her life. Beneath her tentacle, his swollen penis pulsed and jerked. She hoped she wasn't holding his flesh too tight. If she was, he didn't appear to mind, so it must be okay.

She easily floated another tentacle through the cool water and stroked the head of his shaft. His eyes scrunched closed and another volley of bubbles came out of his slightly parted lips. He seemed to be enjoying what she was doing to him. Instincts told her if she kept up the pressure, he would come. So, she backed off. She wanted him to come inside her. Wanted his seed stored inside *her* so that any predator Octo would smell his seed and know she was taken.

She realized she wasn't worried about anything anymore. There was no care. Just a need for pleasure.

As she continued stroking his cockhead, he let go of her waist, reached out with his two upper tentacles and curled them like bondage ropes around her breasts. The pressure was incredible. His suction cups stuck to her flesh, and the tentacles held her breasts until they were firm and plump. The thin tips of his tentacles stroked her nipples until sensations whipped along tender nerve endings. She quivered and creamed. She could smell herself as her aromatic cream splashed into the currents.

Deep in the back of her mind, she sensed her scent could bring danger back to them, but she couldn't stop creaming. She needed the pleasure. Needed him to mate with her. Needed his sperm inside of her.

Miranda wanted to be lost in the frenzy that was quickly building inside her. Every nerve ending in her body screamed to be touched. She tensed with awareness as two tentacles smoothed up along her inner legs again. They were heading toward her core. She trembled with anticipation and a dizzying need for penetration swept over her as one of his tentacle tips prodded against her vaginal opening and the other nudged against her tight sphincter.

She reached out with the third of her four tentacles and cupped the back of his head. Boldly, she urged his head closer to hers and then she fused her lips over his hot mouth. Her senses burst with pleasure.

Gray tasted wonderful. Like salt and male arousal and passion. He kissed her back. Hard. His mouth seared against her lips until they were on fire. Need surged through her. The tentacle at her vagina stretched inside her. It was smooth and thick and felt very different from his cock. Much bigger!

Her vaginal muscles quivered and throbbed around his pulsing flesh. He withdrew and quickly thrust the tentacle into her again. As he pulled out, the other tentacle pushed into her anus. A bite of pain swept through her at the incredible pressure. She tensed and moaned into his mouth.

He kissed her harder and the tentacles wrapped around her breasts tightened wonderfully. He withdrew the tentacle from her ass. Then he plunged his other appendage into her pussy again. She gasped as her vision darkened, and her pussy gripped the impalement. Tremors rocked through her.

Gray slid the other tentacle into her ass again, this time more forcefully. It didn't hurt, but the pressure was unbelievable. He withdrew, and then bucked his hips, thrusting into her ass again. His length was superb as he drove his flesh so deep inside of her, she fought to breathe.

He withdrew. His kisses become more desperate and frantic. Her senses whirled. He unwrapped the tentacles from her breasts, and then he wrapped them around her thighs.

He held Miranda's thighs wide open and she writhed as he thrust a tentacle into her pussy and another one into her ass, both at the same time. She struggled against the restraints as his succulent flesh drove in and out of her. The sharp, almost painful orgasm snapped into her like live wires.

She convulsed and jerked in a frenzy as his steely flesh continued to invade her. Her muscles throbbed and clenched around him. Pleasure scalded her. She strained against the restraints and kissed him harder. The pleasure was never-ending.

Suddenly he slipped a tentacle from her and moved closer. His tentacle slipped around her neck like a collar. He held her there. He owned her.

Then he bucked his hips and thrust his cock deep into her. The intensity of her arousal increased. She twisted and arched against him as his cock and tentacle fell into a wicked double-penetration rhythm. The sensations grew stronger and stronger until fire consumed her.

His tentacles tightened around her thighs and inside her ass. His penis throbbed and thickened and then she shuddered as her vagina milked him of his sperm.

They fucked that way for most of the night, before exhaustion made them stop.

Intertwined in each other's tentacles, they drifted along the ocean current, staring into each other's eyes. She loved Gray's eyes. She easily got lost in the beautiful glowing gray color with the gold flecks. She knew she should reach out and grab some fish to eat, but that would mean breaking this magnetic embrace and that was the last thing she wanted to do.

GRAY HELPED MIRANDA out of the water, moments after she turned back into human form. Her gorgeous naked ass beckoned to him as she climbed the ladder in front of him. Double penetrating her had been the most spectacular experience he'd ever shared with a female. He'd slept with a couple of Octo females when he'd been younger, but it had just been sex. He'd slept with a handful of human women too, but they didn't like it when he disappeared at night, and he'd never trusted them enough to explain why, so those relationships hadn't lasted too long.

Miranda was different. She was the *one*. She was his mate and suddenly he didn't care if Jack approved or not. But he was still going to tell her father his intentions. He owed that much to Jack, despite Miranda's anger and disapproval on the subject.

"I'm so surprised we didn't lose the yacht," she said as she stepped barefoot onto the deck. She laughed and twirled happily, and Gray's cock hardened as he watched her.

Man, did she not understand how he reacted whenever she was in naked form? An uncontrollable savage need to take her again rocked through him. It was unbelievably difficult to stand here and watch her as she began to dance while naked on the deck.

He did a quick survey of their surroundings, noted the yacht wasn't moving. He'd check the anchor situation later. He saw no other vessels out on the water, nor any sign of houses or people along the shoreline. They were safe from prying eyes.

Suddenly she turned and caught him watching her. Her demeanor immediately changed. Her blue eyes darkened with a wild sexual look and a powerful desire to fuck her burned through him. He was about to step toward her when a sensual smile tilted her lips. Her smile made his heart catch fire. He dared not breathe, for it was the most pleasant sensation he'd ever experienced.

Slowly, she shook her head as if to indicate he shouldn't move. He watched her as she closed her eyes. She raised her arms and ran her hands through the slick wet strands of her hair. She began to sway her hips in a sensual rhythm, dancing to a tune of music only she could hear.

His mind shattered as he watched her dance. His legs melted as his hungry gaze wandered over her beautiful human curves.

Last night, his Octo form had mated her to him. Now, his human side craved to claim her and make her know she belonged to him. Her scent was like a sweet, delicate perfume that seduced his senses and trapped his body. She was like a scorching flame and he, the captured moth drawn to her.

He ached so much he could barely walk across the deck to her. His hand shook as he reached up to touch her left nipple. She whimpered as he pinched it and then rubbed it between his thumb and forefinger. Immediately the rose-colored bud hardened.

"I feel so alive. I've never felt so alive," she whispered softly.

She kept dancing in front of him. Her eyelashes fluttered. Her eyelids drooped and then her eyes closed. She swayed her hips and her fingers sifted through the strands of her hair.

He knew exactly what she was talking about. He felt the same way. It was as if he'd been asleep forever and then he'd awakened and had been brought into a world of tremendous desire.

He lifted his other hand and then cupped both her breasts. A soft keening sound drifted between her slightly parted lips. A siren's sound. Sweet and alluring and irresistible. He continued to hold her breasts in his palms and then lowered his head. He sucked her left nipple until it beaded and hardened against his mouth.

She gasped sweetly and shuddered. Her breathing grew hard and fast. He wished he could calm her, make this last, but the aching hardness between his legs was extraordinarily insistent. His shaft begged him to bury it deep inside her tight channel. Pleaded to claim her human form just as frantically as he'd claimed her Octo form.

He sucked on one nipple and then moved to the other. He loved the way she whimpered as he laved his tongue around her areole and nipped her sensitive flesh. Finally, her arms descended onto his shoulders.

"Fuck me," she whispered. Her voice was tight and barely restrained.

He let go and lifted his head. Want seared across her face. He felt it scream through him too. There was no need for foreplay this time. His need to claim her tossed all self-control to the wind.

Gray grabbed Miranda's hips and held her steady. He waited only long enough for her to curl her hands over his shoulders and as they both looked down between their bodies, he watched his cock disappear inside her. He withdrew and thrust into her again. She yelped and instantly exploded into a frenzy of shudders. Fire lanced his shaft as she clenched his flesh. Her vaginal muscles wrapped so tightly around him that pleasure rocketed along the length of his shaft and seared into his balls and belly. He gritted his teeth as he shuddered violently and saw stars as they burst behind his eyes.

Holy Octoposeidon!

He withdrew and then thrust into her again. Miranda pulled at his shoulders, and he moved against her, his mouth melting over her lips. Gray kept up the frantic pace, pistoning and rocking into her over and over again. Driving their pleasure higher and higher as they continued to convulse and shudder against each other.

Finally, he could hold back no longer and shot his release deep inside her, ignoring the warning that he could very well be making her with child. He didn't care. She belonged to him. There was no doubt in his mind.

His.

He held her as the spasms began to weaken. Held her as they stood on the deck, the early-morning breeze caressing their naked flesh and the spectacular sunshine splashing warmth over them as it broke over the horizon.

Gray wanted to bring her to another orgasm, but then he suddenly froze. Movement at the edge of his vision caught his attention. He peered over Miranda's shoulder and discovered that a white speed craft was quickly arrowing toward them. The boat was about two miles or so away, but instincts told him whoever was on that boat was looking for them.

"Miranda, get dressed. We've got company."

She immediately frowned. She turned and squinted into the early morning dawn.

"Who do you think it is?" she asked as he withdrew from her.

"Don't know, but whoever it is, they're in one hell of a hurry to get here."

MIRANDA HURRIEDLY DRESSED in a floral sundress, slid on some sandals and then met Gray up on deck. He'd slipped on a pair of black shorts and a white loose-fitting shirt that billowed up behind him like a sail in the sea breeze. Alarm raced through her as she spied the dark outline of the handle of a gun pressed against the small of his back, shoved into the waistband of his shorts. Was he expecting trouble? Had her scent attracted danger?

Her alarm quickly diffused when she recognized the couple in the speedboat.

"It's Calder and Catalina!" she called out.

She'd met Cat only once but recognized her immediately. She was a beautiful Octoposeidon female and such a nice woman. Miranda was thrilled they had come out to meet them. When Catalina saw them, she began to wave frantically. She appeared quite happy to see them. Calder, on the other hand, wore quite the disapproving scowl.

Uh oh. It looked like something was up.

Chapter Six

"Where the hell have you two been? We've been trying to hail you on the radio all night?" Calder growled after he and Catalina had boarded. His green eyes flashed with both anger and concern as he shook Gray's hand in greeting.

"Oh, ignore his bad manners. He's just grumpy from lack of sleep," Catalina said.

Cat was a striking woman with sparkling blue eyes and shoulder-length wavy auburn hair. Tentacle earrings dangled from her ear lobes, and she wore a gorgeous sleeveless navy-blue dress with a middy collar and white tie. Cute tattoos of various sea life figures were prominent on both her arms, signifying her love of tattoos. She was also an experienced tattoo artist.

She smiled at Miranda, opened her arms, and wiggled her fingers.

"Come here, give me a hug. I want to make sure I am not dreaming this reunion."

Miranda laughed at Cat's choice of words. She stepped into the other woman's embrace and into a warm hug.

"I was so worried something bad happened to you two. I can see now we were just jumping to conclusions," Cat said.

"Why wasn't she answering?"

Calder had turned to Gray to question him. But Gray ignored him and gazed at Miranda over Cat's shoulder. His gaze was so possessive and so heated that Miranda trembled at the intensity.

Catalina let her go.

"What's wrong? You're shaking?" she said with a frown.

"I'm fine. Seriously. Never felt better. You didn't have to come all this way. Goodness, your wedding is in a couple of days. You must have tons still to do."

Cat grinned. "Oh, I should take this opportunity to apologize for the last-minute invitation. Calder proposed rather suddenly and well anyway, everything is ready. We're well organized. We had originally hired an Octo wedding planner, but she had so many ideas."

"We dropped her like a hot potato. She had *too* many ideas, if you ask me," Calder grumbled but he winked teasingly at Miranda.

"Calder's right. If we had waited to be married and listened to all her ideas, we would be a hundred years old. So, we agreed on a fast and simple ceremony with family and close friends."

"Friends like you two. I'm glad you both are okay," Calder said. He stepped forward and gave Miranda a quick hug.

"We were...occupied, last night. Miranda decided to turn when I was already in the water. But she kept her head, and she did great," Gray said softly.

"Oh, my goodness!" Shock splashed over Catalina's face.

Calder remained silent, but Miranda did notice an interesting, knowing look pass between the two males.

"Oh, sweetie. Come, let's go and make something for everyone to eat. You must be starved." Catalina didn't wait for an answer as she suddenly grabbed Miranda by her hand and pulled her into the nearby salon.

"You two men stay there. We'll call you when breakfast is ready," Catalina said to the guys.

When they reached the salon, Cat instructed Miranda to have a seat.

"You must be famished. You poor dear," she cooed as she opened several cupboards and started dragging out some packaged food that Miranda had brought along for the trip.

"Actually, I'm okay. We ate fish. Lots of fish."

Cat hesitated and peered over her shoulder at her. The other woman's cheeks were a bit flushed.

"Then you must be tired. I know when I first turned, I was confused and tired. Calder and I...um...well, let's say it was a confusing time."

Miranda smiled. Warmth embraced her heart at Catalina's concern.

"Actually, I did a lot of research on the Octo site, so I knew what to expect. Kind of knew, anyway. I thought I was going to be able to handle anything, but when it happened, it was just shocking to go through something like that. I was stunned at first and then my instincts took over."

Cat giggled. "Oh yeah, instincts are quite nice where males are concerned."

Miranda patted the bench seat beside her, eager now to get the lowdown on Cat's first Octo experience with Calder.

In a second, the other woman had joined her. Before long Miranda was blushing at how Calder and Catalina had met through Cat's mobile tattoo service. He'd contacted her and had requested a tentacle tattoo on his cock, and Cat hadn't even known she was an Octo when Calder had started to pursue her.

By the time Catalina had finished her story, Miranda was glad she hadn't been kept in the dark about her heritage as Catalina had been. Cat's confession made a proud confidence weave through her. For the first time in her life, Miranda realized how lucky she was to have her overprotective dad and that he *had* told her about the Octoposeidon and about her mother being one. And that there was a chance that Miranda would turn.

Suddenly, she really liked who she was and how she had turned out. She liked herself. A lot.

"SO, YOU HAVE YOURSELF a female now," Calder chuckled as he slapped Gray on his bare back while they walked along the sandy California beach. Calder had suggested the two of them get off the yacht and get in some walking because, as he confessed to Gray, he was a nervous wreck about marrying Cat.

So, Gray had returned his gun to the safety of a locked cabinet, ditched his shirt and both of them had jumped overboard into the pristine warm waters and swam to the sandy shore.

It wasn't until now that he realized Calder's reason to leave the yacht was just an excuse to get the scoop on Gray's relationship with Miranda.

"If you want to know if we've mated, the answer is yes," Gray frankly stated.

To his surprise, Calder's facial expression remained neutral.

"And what are your intentions toward her? I don't want her hurt, Gray. She's inexperienced and she never really wanted to become an Octo..."

Irritation shot through Gray, and he abruptly stopped walking. He clenched his fists and resisted the urge to punch Calder in the nose. Sure, he understood Calder's concern. For all the guy knew from past experiences, Miranda and Gray hated each other. Hell, everyone knew they fought like cats and dogs.

"Things are different now. She's mine," he growled the last word to make sure Calder understood. In the way Calder's eyes widened, he did.

"Then I don't know how this will come across, but now that she has turned, she'd going to need protection. I smelled her scent forty miles down the coastline. That's how I could easily locate you two. She's got a very strong trail, Gray."

"I'll protect her."

"How? By keeping her hidden in that Alaskan inlet like her father has been doing?"

"It's worked so far."

"Only because she wasn't scenting. Now that she is, every Octo male can smell her and follow her back. And if you're not around to protect her...it's happened to your consortium. You should know more than anyone how much females need to be protected."

Gray shivered as he remembered smelling the blood drifting along the currents. The fear that had twisted his gut. Panicking and swimming right into an ambush.

"Why are you telling me this, Calder? Do you want us to join a consortium? They didn't protect my family then and they can't protect us now. Having so many females all in one place just makes their scents stronger. My sisters have decided to live alone, and they've managed fine with their decision. Miranda and I can do the same."

"As I said, I could smell her. There are any number of Octo males out there who won't respect that she's taken."

"We'll take precautions from here on out." Although he had no idea what those precautions would entail. There really was no one-hundred-percent protection for a female Octoposeidon, unless they lived in the middle of nowhere like Jack had been doing with Miranda.

Calder nodded tightly. "Well, Catalina and I formed a consortium."

This was news to him.

"We just formed it when we discovered there were several Octoposeidon in the area of my marina. You both are welcome to come and live nearby. The males take turns patrolling at night in the oceans so we can keep the females as safe as possible. Everyone gets a tattoo — a brand, if you will — signifying they belong to a certain consortium."

Calder pointed to the large black tattoo with an intricate design on his left shoulder and biceps.

"It's the brand of our consortium. When we turn into Octo form at night, the tattoo glows. It's how we can tell quickly if an Octo belongs to our group or not."

"I heard that the Octo society was adopting a tattoo procedure." Gray said as he inspected the design. It looked impressive.

"Yes, the idea came from Cat and me. She uses special inks that glow gently beneath the depths. Not bright enough so that an enemy can see from a distance, but just enough so if one of the bodyguards gets close, they can tell if the Octo is friend or foe. And there's an added benefit for when we're in human form. We've discovered the tattoos get brighter a few minutes before we even feel the need to turn. When you're in the human world, it's always good to know ahead of time so you can make your excuses and disappear. Even a couple of minutes is a big help."

Gray nodded. He realized that maybe Calder was right. Miranda needed major protection, and he might not be able to give it to her. He sure didn't want to lose her because of his doubts about consortiums.

"The consortium and tattoo sound like a good idea. But I can't give you a decision one way or the other unless I discuss this with Miranda."

Calder nodded. He looked somewhat relieved. Then he smiled and nodded toward the yacht.

"The women are hailing us."

Gray looked over at the yacht bobbing in the sparkling aqua-blue waters and saw Miranda and Catalina waving to them.

"It looks like breakfast is ready. Want to race to the yacht? Last one there does the dishes?"

Calder didn't answer, as he was already diving into the water. A moment later, his head popped out of the water, and he waved to Gray.

"Last one there does the dishes!"

Son of a bitch! He had heard him!

Gray dove into the ocean, but Calder already had such a head start that Gray knew he was the one who would be doing the dishes. But that was okay. It would give him some time to think about what Calder had said. He'd made some good points about the dangers of being Octoposeidon and of having a female to protect now. He wondered how Miranda would react when he suggested they move down here to California.

"YOU AREN'T SAYING ANYTHING," Gray said as he studied Miranda.

They had followed Cat and Calder in the yacht along the coastline to a secluded beach several miles from Calder's marina. The two of them had enjoyed a dinner of buttered lobster. Over a shrimp salad, he'd mentioned what Calder had said about joining the consortium here.

"That's because there's nothing to say," she replied with a grimace.

"What do you think?" he prodded.

She shook her head and shrugged.

"About?"

Man, why was she making this so difficult for him?

"We've been careless out here all alone. Now that you've turned, your scent is very active. Bad things can happen. Octo males are desperate."

She frowned and an uneasiness zipped through him.

"Exactly how desperate are they, Gray?"

His gut twisted at the snarl in her voice. What had he said wrong now? He picked up her irritation and it snapped through him as well.

"Do I need to spell it out for you? Do I need to tell you what happened to the women in my consortium? The females were kidnapped, Miranda. Taken against their will. Some were killed because they fought. We can't go to the human law. They don't know we exist. And Octo laws are like the humans' Wild West days at best. My sisters live alone in isolation. They want nothing to do with the Octoposeidon race. They barely interact with the human race. They rarely see each other or me because they live in fear. I don't want that for you or for us, Miranda."

"You didn't answer my question, Gray," she said softly.

Gray blinked in surprise. She acted as if he hadn't even said anything.

"Question? What the hell are you talking about?"

"How desperate are you, Gray?"

What the fuck?

"Are you screwing me because there's no other female around? Or are you doing me for another reason?"

A dark pink blushed her cheeks and she seemed fidgety. Her hands were knotted on the table in front of her and she was nibbling on her bottom lip as if she was worried about something. Realization hit him like a ton of bricks. Damn, but the woman had balls. Damn sexy as hell cute balls.

"What do you want me to say, Miranda? That I am so desperate and that's why I picked you because I couldn't find a pretty-enough Octo?"

She visibly tensed at his teasing words. Was she serious? Did she not know how attracted he was to her?

Gray shook his head. It appeared she had no clue. Then, perhaps he needed to show her.

He stood. Her eyes widened in surprise as he slipped his fingers beneath the waistband of his shorts and slid them down past his hips. His cock sprang free, and it was a relief to have it out of captivity.

"Do you think it is fun for me to go around with a hard-on whenever I smell you?"

He stepped out of his shorts in front of her. She blinked at him, her cheeks flushing a deeper pink.

"I've wanted you since I can remember, Miranda. First, when you were younger, it was a protective instinct. Then when you got older, it turned into something else. I admit I tried to deny it. Your dad gave me shelter and a job and I didn't want to admit to him or to myself that what I felt for you had turned serious. So, I teased you to keep you mad at me. To keep you away from me."

She shook her head slowly, a look of wonder on her face.

"And to answer your question. I'm screwing you because I want you to be my mate. You are the only female for me. I wouldn't be having unprotected sex with you, as we had earlier, unless I wanted babies with you. Lots of babies."

She made a cute little O with her lips and understanding sparkled in her eyes. He came around the table and held his hand out to her. She slipped her trembling fingers against his palm, and he held her hand gently yet firmly at the same time as he pulled her to a standing position in front of him.

"You belong to me, Randi." He hoped his voice was firm enough so she would believe him. He also knew he could talk until he was blue in the face, because talk was cheap. She needed action, and he would give her plenty.

STUNNED DISBELIEF SUNK slowly past Miranda's insecurities. She couldn't believe what Gray had just confessed. He wanted babies with her. She'd thought about the unprotected sex they'd had earlier. It was one of the reasons she needed to make sure that he wasn't just fucking her because she was convenient. She wanted to make sure he was serious. It appeared he truly did want her. He'd wanted her and he'd kept it hidden behind his teasing? She thought back. It must be at least several years that they'd been at each other's throats.

Son-of-a-bitch.

Now, he stood in front of her in his naked glory, baring himself to her. The vulnerability in his eyes was unmistakable. She had no choice but to bare herself to him. In every sense of the word.

"I have to admit, you did a pretty good job at keeping me off balance. I was mad at you more times than I was glad to know you. But secretly I did fantasize about you. Masturbated to visions of you...like the other night."

His sharp inhalation of breath made her hesitate. But she'd gone this far, she may as well continue.

"It seemed the angrier I was at you, the wilder my orgasms..."

He cut off her words by fusing his mouth over hers.

Oh, my. The Octo knew how to kiss.

"Shut up, Miranda," he whispered against her mouth. He let go of her hands and she shivered as his fingers touched the hem of her sundress. She lifted her arms, and he yanked the dress up and over her head. To her surprise, he tossed her dress into the wind. It fluttered like a sail and billowed over the edge of the yacht.

"Hey! That's one of my favorite sundresses!" she complained.

"We'll get it later. Right now, I want you naked and I want to show you one of my favorite positions," he growled.

He slipped his hand into hers and led her to a deck table near the stern of the yacht.

"Turn around and face the ocean," he instructed.

His voice dripped with arousal, and she could feel it sift through her like a magnificent wave.

"We won't be needing this either," he muttered. Fingers slipped beneath the waistband of her panties, and he tugged it down over her hips and down her legs. She stepped out of them, and she kicked them to the edge. A burst of wind picked her underwear up and it sailed out onto the ocean.

"Hey! Those are my favorite panties on you," he whispered.

She grinned. "We'll get it later."

His hot palms splayed against her upper back, and he gently pushed her until her upper torso was on the table and her nipples were rubbing against the coarse tabletop.

"It's a nice view," she whispered as she gazed out at the white seagulls swooping over gently rolling turquoise waves.

"The view is better back here," he growled. His palms slid down her back and he gently caressed her ass cheeks. "Spread your legs for me, sweetheart."

She widened her feet and a second later, she gasped as he palmed her pussy.

"I love how easily you cream for me," he whispered.

"I love the way you touch me," she whispered back. It was true. Whether he was gentle or rough, she enjoyed whatever he did to her.

She flushed as he roughly ground his palm against her clit. The pressure sparked wicked shudders through her. He let go of her and then thrust a finger into her wet vagina. He withdrew it quickly. Then he began a fast-paced rub over her clit using her cream as lube.

Within seconds, a flaming need snapped through her. Her breathing quickened and she tensed as erotic awareness splashed over her in tumultuous waves. Her body tightened and her pleasure mounted. She burned and her hips swayed with desperate need. She ached like crazy for him.

"Gray!" she gasped as her muscles frantically clenched around empty air. She needed him to fill her. Now!

She whimpered with frustration as his finger left her clit. A second later, he grabbed her hips and then thrust deep inside her. She jerked her hips against his hands and shattered into a volley of convulsions. Her vaginal muscles quivered around his steely erection as he pumped into her with quick, solid strokes.

Within seconds, his cries of release joined hers and the cries of the seagulls swooping around the yacht.

"DO YOU, CALDER, TAKE Catalina to be your wedded wife, to have and to hold from this day forward, for better, for worse, for richer, for poorer, in sickness and in health, to love and to cherish forever, for as long as you both shall live?" the presenter asked.

"I do," Calder said in a strong voice.

He stood proud and tall wearing a light gray tuxedo with black tie. Catalina looked stunning standing beside him. She wore a breathtaking mermaid-style white wedding gown. The dress was cut slim through the bodice and hip areas and flared out below. She had a sprig of white baby's breath tucked behind her left ear.

Both of them stood beneath a white rose-covered arbor with the turquoise ocean as a backdrop. Miranda's breath caught at how intense the couple gazed into each other's eyes. It was as if they were the only two people in the entire world and the thirty or so friends and family watching the ceremony were not even there.

Because Octoposeidon had no religion, various human traditions were adjusted and adapted to whatever the bride and groom wanted. Catalina and Calder had opted for the traditional wedding vows but with no wedding rings exchanged. Instead, the two had gotten identical wedding rings tattooed onto intimate parts of their body. No one knew where. As Catalina had whispered to Miranda earlier this morning, it was an area where only Calder could see.

"Do you, Catalina, take Calder to be your wedded husband, to have and to hold from this day forward, for better, for worse, for richer, for poorer, in sickness and in health, to love and to cherish forever, for as long as you both shall live?"

"I do," Catalina whispered.

"I now pronounce you husband and wife. You may kiss the bride."

Miranda smiled as Gray slipped his fingers against her palm and gently squeezed her hand. They had decided that they would remain here in California with Calder and Catalina. They had spoken to her dad over the phone yesterday. Miranda had broken the news that she had gone through the Change, and she was with Gray now. To her surprise, her father had taken it rather well, even laughing and congratulating her and telling her she had picked an excellent partner.

When her father had asked to speak with Gray, Miranda had tensed. But Gray had taken the phone and told her father that he would take good care of Miranda by keeping her under the protection of the consortium in the area. Dad had told Gray he thought that was a good idea and had given Gray his blessing. Gray had been smiling ever since.

Jack had even mentioned that perhaps he might close up shop and come down to California and they could all work together again. Miranda and Gray had eagerly agreed.

Earlier today, they'd delivered the yacht to the owner, who had been ecstatic. The rest of the payment for the yacht was safely tucked away in their business bank account. They were already searching for accommodations suitable for a yacht-building business here.

During the reception, they danced until the urge to go to the ocean grew so strong that they had to leave the party. They didn't have too far to go though, as the reception was on the beach.

Calder and Cat had several human friends who had no idea that they were shifters, so the party was still in full swing with several humans. By the time Gray and Miranda left, all the Octos had already discreetly disappeared.

They opted to walk up the beach. Calder had indicated there was a safe and secluded area near his marina where he and Cat swam at night. Cat and Calder wouldn't be using the area for a few nights, as the newlyweds had taken Calder's houseboat out on the ocean and they would be honeymooning somewhere up the coast.

While they walked, Miranda studied the new tattoo on Gray's left shoulder and biceps. The tattoo was identical to the one Calder wore and as far as Miranda was concerned it made Gray look sexier than ever. A matching tattoo had been placed on her Miranda's right shoulder. Right now, both of their tattoos were glowing a gorgeous midnight blue, signifying they would be Turning within minutes.

After they undressed, Miranda and Gray hid their clothing in some dense bushes. Then, while holding hands, they waded into the mild ocean. Calder had assured them that they would be safe here because Octoposeidon males took turns patrolling the area and soon Gray would be joining their ranks to help.

It was a good feeling knowing they had less to fear. She'd noticed, too, that Gray had become more relaxed since their decision of staying. In turn, she felt confident that he would be safe and she felt more at ease too.

As they gazed out across the ocean and waited to Turn, they watched the sun dip behind the horizon. As it disappeared, it cast a golden hue over the glass-like surface.

"Beautiful view tonight," she whispered.

"Yes, very beautiful," Gray's soft voice made her gaze at him. He was staring at her with vulnerable love shining in his eyes. The sight made her tremble with excitement.

If someone had told her a little over a week ago that she would be having sex with Gray and dreaming about a life with him in California, she would have called them nuts. Yet here they were. And she couldn't be happier.

The End

Spunky Girl Publishing Catalog

Jan Springer ~ Erotic Romance

Naughty Girl Desires
Jan Springer

FOUR CONTEMPORARY ROMANCES with a naughty edge and a snap of suspense. Contains: Jade's Fantasy (Kidnap Fantasies 1), The Biker and The Bride, Sinderella Sexy, & Nice Girl Naughty

Jade's Fantasy (Kidnap Fantasies 1)

IN THE LAND OF THE rich and famous, Kidnap Fantasies is the answer to discreet naughty downtime.

When ex-downhill skier Jade's two sisters give her a Kidnap Fantasies questionnaire, Jade is aroused at the prospect of having no-strings fun in the sun with a stranger whose only job would be to fulfill her every intimate fantasy. Although she knows she's too shy to send it in, she secretly pours her deepest wishes into the questionnaire.

Soon the questionnaire mysteriously vanishes, and Jade's fantasy man appears on her luxury yacht in the form of a sexy handy man who gives her an intimate toy-filled holiday she'll never forget.

The Biker and The Bride

WRAPPED IN RED-HOT lust for revenge, Avery plots to murder the man responsible for the death of her son.

Her plans are dashed when her ex-husband whisks her away on his motorcycle to the rustic Canadian wilderness cabin, they'd once honeymooned.

Police detective, Mason is fighting for Avery's love with everything he has.

Armed with whipped cream, handcuffs and his undying devotion, Mason vows he will make Avery love again.

But it's only a matter of time before the man she'd planned to kill hunts them down...

Sinderella Sexy

BY DAY, SHE'S A DEDICATED gynecologist.

By night, Dr. Ella Cinder, escapes reality by secretly performing in her own version of Cinderella, aptly re-titled Sinderella.

When sexy colleague Dr. Roarke Stephenson shows up in the Sinderella audience on the same night her Prince Charming stands her up, Ella seizes the opportunity to make Roarke into her Prince Charming for one carnal night of extremely naughty fun in front of an audience.

But at the strike of midnight, Ella knows she must face the harsh reality that Roarke must never learn her secret life and they can never be together again. Until then, she'll make sure he'll never forget their night of sensual play...

Nice Girl Naughty

BLIND SINCE NINETEEN, Summer has blossomed into a famous wood carver.

When she's almost killed by a serial killer, she's whisked away to a secluded wilderness cabin by the man she once secretly loved.

Summer can't get enough of touching professional bodyguard Nick Cassidy's thick, powerful muscles and all those other hard, yummy male body parts that she has always longed to explore.

For years Nick has stayed away from his best friend's kid sister, nice girl Summer. Now he's back and sweeping his gorgeous redhead into the naughty cravings he's always had for her. With passion blinding him, Nick doesn't realize their hideout isn't safe—until it's too late.

Vampira
Jan Springer

VAMPIRA – A CLOSE-knit clique of female vampires who have escaped the tyranny of their clans. Vampira – a feminine faction who live undetected among the humans and where mating with males is strictly forbidden...

Includes 4 sizzling ménage vampire erotic romances ~ Sweet Heat (#1), Dark Heat (#2), Wet Heat (#3), Crimson Heat (#4).

Sweet Heat ~ Vampira 1

Running from an arranged marriage, Juliette Dárques' hides within Vampira, a secret clique of female vampires who live among humans and have sworn off sex with males.

Julie thought she was safe until scorching dreams leave her craving every hot, pulsing inch of the two vamps newly hired at the factory she owns. Every night they set her fangs on fire, as they sandwich her between their strong, naked bodies, whisking her into a world of forbidden ecstasy.

Caleb and Zander have always shared a unique bond, which includes the need to share their females. Lately, they've been hungering for Julie...and they plan on seducing her out of her dreams and into their arms.

Dark Heat ~ Vampira 2

WARRIOR QUEEN MEGAN Bloodrayne was betrayed by her two mates. Fleeing them, she hides within Vampira, a secret coven of vampires who live undetected among the humans.

Recaptured, Megan learns she's been framed for crimes she did not commit. Her mates, kings Christian and Zane, believe she may be a traitor, and they'll try *anything* to get the truth out of her.

Megan's got a secret, and she'll do anything to keep it, including enduring scorching sessions of red-hot sensual pleasure.

Wet Heat ~ Vampira 3

TORMENTED AND ABUSED.

As a Blood Slave, Mati Smith craved freedom. After escaping her owners and near death, she was nursed back to health by two sexy Italian male vamps. Realizing she'd fallen in love with them and had put their lives in peril, she disappeared into the human world, creating the powerful coven Vampira, where females on the run seek sanctuary and where mating with males is forbidden.

Dangerous cravings.

When Mati's two lovers reconnect their mind link, she craves physical pleasure like never before. She seeks relief at Vamp's Bordella, where, under the seductive hands of two pleasure males, she defies Vampira and finds searing satisfaction.

Mind seduction.

Giovanni and Paolo have lured Mati to the bordella in order to claim her. Will she disappear again when she realizes she's been tricked? Or will she finally submit to the scorching desires the three share? If Gio and Paolo get their way, their long-lost love will be theirs forever...

Crimson Heat ~ Vampira 4

VAMPIRE LISBETH CROWE has done her best to put her past as Satin, the Queen's favorite blood slave, behind her—even if it has meant leaving three delicious, devoted lovers behind.

Escaping Russia and the Crimson Clan and becoming an American entrepreneur has helped Lisbeth stay safe, as has joining the powerful, all-female Vampira coven, which prohibits its members from becoming involved with men. But when Lisbeth models in a charity fashion show as a favor to a friend, one of the Queen's evil minions sees her—and begins scheming to return her to the wicked monarch who loved to dine on her so much.

Jaymes, Tristan and Luca have longed for their beloved Satin for decades—and after hearing of her whereabouts, they rush to reach her before the Queen's henchmen can. Racing against time, they track her to a desolate hideaway, resuming their long-denied love affair and are determined to fight to the death to protect their female.

Her Sexy Cowboys
The First Five Books in the Cowboys Online ~ Moose Ranch Series
Jan Springer
A Canadian Contemporary Ménage Romance m/f/m/m Series

JENNIFER JANE (JJ) Watson has spent the past ten Christmases in a maximum-security prison.

The last thing she expects is to get early parole, along with a job on a remote Canadian cattle ranch serving dinners to three of the sexiest cowboys she's ever met!

Rafe, Brady and Dan thought they were getting a couple of male ex-cons to help out around their secluded ranch, but instead they get an attractive and very appealing female.

In the wilds of Northern Ontario, Canada, female companionship is rare.

It's a good thing the three men like to share...

They're dominating, sexy-as-sin and they fill JJ with the hottest intimate fantasies she's ever had. Suddenly she's craving cowboy ménages and wishing for something she knows she can never have...a happily ever after.

INCLUDES COWBOYS FOR Christmas, Cowboys In Her Pocket, Loving Her Cowboys, Cowboys in Her Heart, and Always Her Cowboys. Not included are Her Forever Cowboys, Claiming Her Cowboys, and Rescued by Her Cowboys. More in the works!

Dark Solar

m/f/m/m

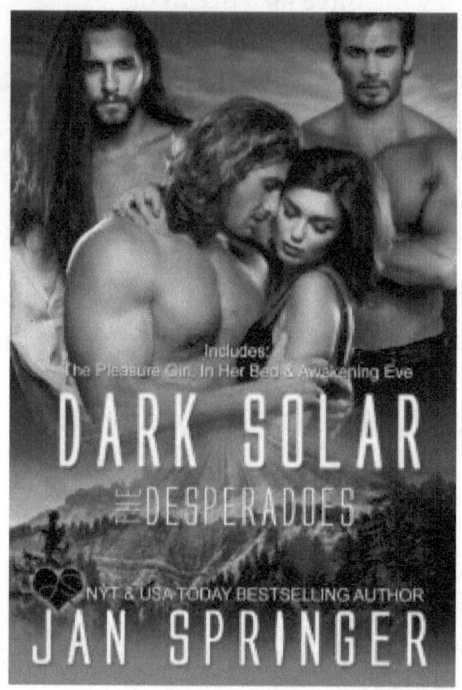

Three book bundle.

SIZZLING HOT REVERSE harem m/f/m/m set in a post-catastrophic aftermath with a western ambiance where solar flares have disintegrated most of the Earth's human population and destroyed electrical grids.

Inside this three-book erotic romance foursome bundle you'll discover strong women forced into a naughty way of life and the sexy outlaw men who love and share them.

These books are full-length, with ménage a quatre, bdsm, pleasure toys and more wickedly delightful adventures that a woman could wish for!

Includes the first three books in The Desperadoes Series:
The Pleasure Girl, In Her Bed, Awakening Eve

The Pleasure Girl
The Desperadoes Series
Book One
Jan Springer

SOLAR FLARES HAVE DISINTEGRATED *most of Earth's human population, frying electrical grids and thrusting everyone into a cold, harsh land where only the strong survive.*

After the catastrophe, Teyla Sutton becomes a pleasure girl, entertaining men on her secluded Canadian farm. When she accommodates dangerous desperado, Logan Leigh and his two friends, Spencer and Cassidy, pleasure becomes addictive beneath their tender touches and their hard, muscular bodies. What she never expects...is to fall in love.

Logan shouldn't allow the pleasure girl into his heart, but he knows it's too late because she's already there. He and his friends have put their lives into danger by hiding out at her farm. They're on the run. They need to leave, yet Logan wants her so much. Dare he risk his heart and their lives to be with her?

Soon Logan, Cassidy and Spencer are whisking Teyla on an exquisite journey into her hottest desires and forbidden fantasies. But when she learns the trio are members of a notorious outlaw gang, can she allow them to stay in her life, or will she send them away forever?

— ◦◦ —

In Her Bed
The Desperadoes Series
Book Two
Jan Springer

A FIERY ERUPTION OF *solar flares disintegrates much of the world's population, fries electrical grids, and throws Earth back into the dark ages. Now, it's a cold, brutal land where only the strong survive.*

Before the Catastrophe, Dr. Elizabeth Brandywine would never have dreamed of surrendering to her wicked needs of being bound, dominated, and shared, but now there's no one left alive to judge her, except herself.

Ethan Durango knows sweet, uptight, sexy Dr. Liz is ready to submit to her secret most intimate needs and he's *always* wanted to share her.

Ethan, Landon, and Tyrell will enjoy pushing Liz past her boundaries until she submits to her naughtiest desires.

Awakening Eve
The Desperadoes Series
Book Three
Jan Springer

A FIERY ERUPTION OF solar flares disintegrates most of Earth's human population, frying electrical grids around the world and thrusting everyone into a cold, harsh land where only the strong survive.

Passionate ménages with some of the fierce men of the Durango gang have always made Eve Wright's body hum with sizzling arousal. Secretly, she loved three men, that is, until she suffered a head injury and forgot them. Now her memory is returning with a carnal vengeance, and she knows of only one way to relieve her naughty frustrations...by returning to the men she once loved.

When Eve shows up at their hideout, Kayne, Riley, and Maddox are pleased she wants them to help her remember what they once shared. Their hot looks, tender touches, and scorching pleasure-pain will leave Eve tangled in an erotic storm that threatens to break her heart and give up a gut-wrenching secret.

Reverse Harem Ménage Amour: Erotic Futuristic Sci-Fi Western Ménage a Quatre Romance, M/F/M/M, post-apocalyptic. Please be aware of some coarse language.

Alpha Outlaws (Books 1-5 Outlaw Lovers)
Post Catastrophe/Sci Fi Erotic Romances
5 Books!!

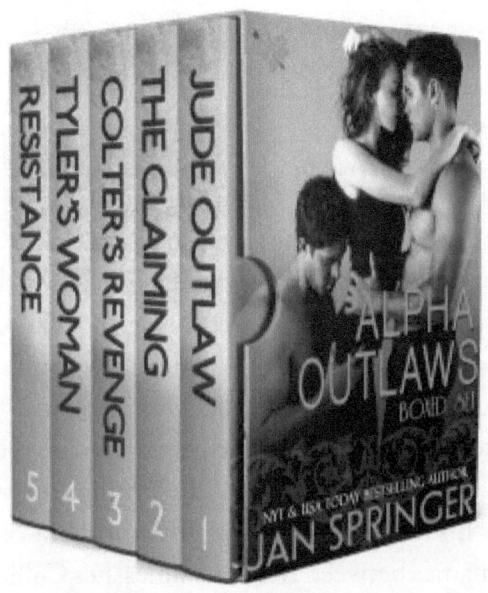

1

In a world gone mad...
A fast-acting virus has killed a majority of the world's female population.
With the creation of The Claiming Law, groups of men suddenly have the
right to claim a female as their sensual property and the sexy Outlaw
brothers are going to declare ownership of the women, they love...any way
they can.

Jude Outlaw
WHEN CATE CALLAHAN learns Jude is coming home from the
Terrorist Wars and is ready to claim her under the new law—with the

---

1. https://janspringerauthor.files.wordpress.com/2010/07/alphaoutlaws_js_box_final.jpg

help of his four brothers—she steals their boat and escapes to the high seas. Unfortunately, her runaway bid for freedom doesn't last long.

Quickly capturing his lover, Jude rekindles the flames and seduces Cate back into his bed.

But Jude holds a secret that could make him lose Cate forever...

PLUS

The Claiming

SEEKING REFUGE FROM the Claiming Law, Callie Callahan hides in a deserted cabin in the Maine woods and is shocked when her ex-flame finds her. She's always craved being in Luke Outlaw's arms. Tasting him. Touching him. Taking him deeply within her. So, what's a girl to do but to delve into the sinful delights he offers.

Luke has finally reunited with the love of his life. He knows there is only one way to keep Callie safe and with him forever. He'll do it with the help of his three brothers and an assortment of naughty toys. Rekindling the flames between them, he unleashes Callie's sensual side, taking her in ways she never dreamed possible, all with the ultimate goal of introducing her to the Outlaw Lovers and The Claiming.

Colter's Revenge

REVENGE BELONGS TO Dr. Colter Outlaw when he unexpectedly reunites with the beautiful woman who broke his heart during the Terrorist Wars. Capturing her, collaring her and holding her against her will, he seduces her, fills her with wicked desires and naughty cravings for a delicious ménage. Fully intent on breaking her heart and walking away, Colter's plans unravel when he submits to the carnal pleasures Ashley gives him so freely.

Colter had told her he loved her. He'd whispered promises of rescue from her life as a slave, but when he'd suddenly disappeared, she'd been devastated. Infected with a version of the X-virus that leaves Ashley Blakely sexually excited on a daily basis, she has come to Pleasure Palace to bid on a cure for her illness. She never expected her Outlaw Lover to be there and screw her plans. Nor did she expect to give him her heart and body so easily...

Tyler's Woman

FOR YEARS TYLER OUTLAW and his best friend, Hunter Brown, endured brutal torture and worse in an overseas terrorist prison. Finally, free of their hell, they return home intent on seducing Laurie into their erotic-filled fantasies.

Laurie Callahan has always experienced red-hot pleasure and passionate love in Tyler Outlaw's arms. But when he's pronounced MIA, presumed dead in the Terrorist Wars, Laurie's world is shattered, and her heart is broken.

Shocked to discover Tyler is alive and he's taken a male lover, Laurie is thrust into a sensual world of sizzling seductions, scorching ménages and the carnal desires that both scarred men crave. But she fears Tyler won't want her when he discovers she's not the same woman he left behind...

****READER CAUTION IS ADVISED Trigger Warning (m/m forced scenes) ****

PLUS~

Resistance

In the near future, a virus has been unleashed, killing a majority of the world's female population, forcing the introduction of the Claiming Law. A law that states men have all the rights and women are sexual property claimable by groups of men.

Fugitive female...

Renegade Resistance leader Reena "Red" Wilde is in for the fight of her life when she experiences an erotic attraction to the two most dangerous men she's ever met.

Black ops assassin...

Months ago, Will "Blade" Smith spent one sizzling evening in the arms of a red-haired seductress. Now she's his next assignment. One look into her gorgeous eyes and he's wrestling his heated cravings for her all over again.

Bounty Hunter...

When Cade Outlaw nabs his bounty, sexy-as-sin Reena Wilde, his profession dictates she's hands-off. But he can't ignore the magnetic sparks between them...or that she is the biggest temptation of his life.

Resistance is futile...

After Reena escapes Cade and Will and falls prey to a band of evil hunters, she's grateful her sexy hunks come to her rescue...and in return, saves their lives. Trapped in a solitary cabin during a wicked snowstorm, she can't resist her two, well-hung studs, nor can she deny they've claimed her heart.

More Collections!

O ther sets by Jan Springer include Her Sexy Cowboys, Dark Solar, Risque Girl Delights, Shades of Ménage, Pleasure Bound, Naughty Girl Desires, Alpha Outlaws, A Touch of Ménage, Shifters by the Sea, Vampira, Intimate Secrets and Merry Menage Kisses.

More Jan Springer stories at:
http://www.janspringer.com

Jasmine Black ~ Erotica without the romance

(a.k.a. Jan Springer writing as Jasmine Black)
Here are some Jasmine Black stories.

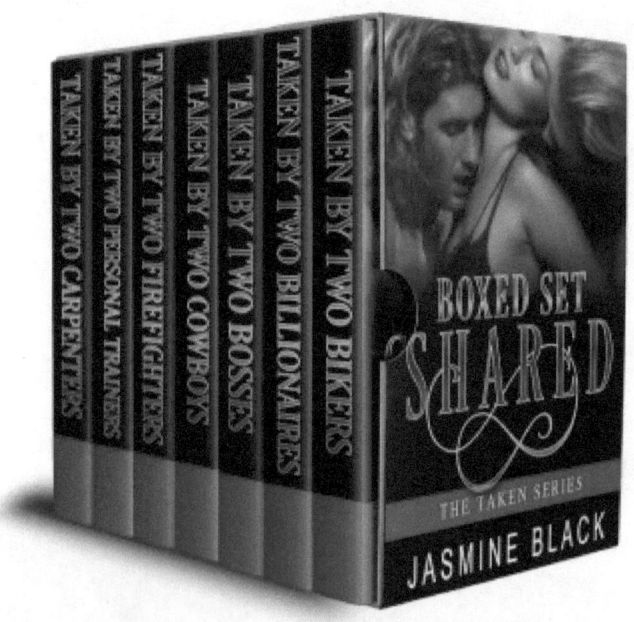

Includes SEVEN EROTIC MENAGES by Jasmine Black ~ Taken by Two Bikers, Taken by Two Billionaires, Taken by Two Bosses, Taken by Two Cowboys, Taken by Two Firefighters, Taken by Two Personal Trainers, Taken by Two Carpenters.

See below for more details!
Taken by Two Bikers
Jasmine Black
When waitress Zoe Miller's car breaks down late one night on a deserted road, she's thankful her biker ex-boyfriend and his best friend come to her rescue...in more ways than one!

Taken By Two Billionaires
Jasmine Black
Jill has always been warned that her gambling lifestyle would get her into trouble. And now she's in trouble.
She's lost a poker game to two very sexy billionaires and they want her as their winnings.
They'll to do her whatever they wish...for an entire year.
On her way to her new life in Italy, while in a white stretch limo, Franco and Gianni will show Jill exactly what it means to be won by two billionaires.

Taken by Two Bosses
Jasmine Black
Trapped in the company elevator, receptionist Carina Chantilli is suddenly at the mercy of her two sexy bosses...

Taken by Two Cowboys
Jasmine Black
Sierra Allan works hard at her late father's horse ranch. When her step-brother adds her handy girl services to a private auction to help

raise money for the failing ranch, she figures there's no harm...but she's stunned when she's "sold" to two sexy cowboys who demand she submit to their dark desires...

Taken by Two Firefighters
Jasmine Black
Firefighter Kendall Farell has always been attracted to the erotic beauty of the hot flames that dance in burning buildings. Her dangerous fetish could cost her her job if anyone ever finds out. When she's caught flirting with fire and rescued from certain death, her two male co-workers want payback in a very naughty way...

Taken by Two Personal Trainers
Jasmine Black
When dancer Chelsea White discovers her lucrative job is in jeopardy, she hires an extreme team to whip her back into physical shape. But her two personal trainers aren't going to give her just any regular gym exercises...

Taken by Two Carpenters
Jasmine Black
A gift certificate from her three besties has Colleen Rue ordering an extravagant pleasure machine from The Sexy Wooden Toy Shoppe, but she quickly discovers that the two well-muscled carpenters have much more in mind than just showing her how the machine works...

Taken by Two Prison Guards

Twenty-three-year-old Madeline "Mad" Madison has quite the temper. She got ten to life in prison due to her getting mad at her late boyfriend and there's only one naughty way she knows of to keep herself calm and she's not getting *that* type of rehabilitation in prison. That is, until she's assigned hard labor on a chain gang and is taken by two prison guards.

Taken by Three Billionaires

Billionaire friends, Liam, Theo and Elijah have just won Princess Isabella in a billionaire card game. Isabella knows exactly what the three men will want from her...she just hadn't expected to have all three of them at once!

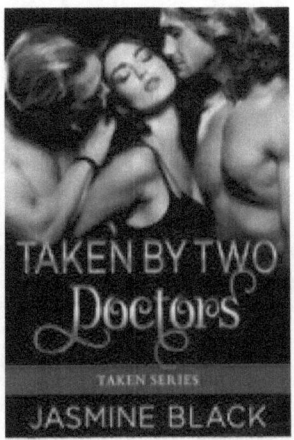

Taken by Two Doctors
A BDSM Medical Fetish Erotica Quickie MFM

Waitress Jean Spelling visits her controversial doctor once a month for some much needed...stress relief. She looks forward to putting her feet up in the stirrups and enjoys Dr. Ball's naughty unconventional treatments. This time when she arrives, she's surprised to discover that she'll be physically examined by two doctors, and they'll prescribe her some much-needed release right there on the examination table!

Ménage series
Taken by Three Bodyguards
Taken by Three Bikers
Taken by Three Billionaires
Taken by Three Doctors
Taken by Three Cowboys
Taken by Three Prison Guards

Taken series.
Taken by Two X-Husbands
Taken by Two Sugar Daddies
Taken by Two Prison Guards
Taken by Two Elves
Taken by Two Mountain Men
Taken by Two Cops
Taken by Two Santas
Taken by Two Lifeguards
Taken by Two Firefighters
Taken by Two Bikers
Taken by Two Billionaires
Taken by Two Bosses
Taken by Two Cowboys
Taken by Two Personal Trainers
Taken by Two Carpenters

Jasmine Black Website ~ http://www.jasmine-black.com

Here are ways we can connect:

Jasmine Black Website at http://janspringerauthor.wordpress.com/jasmine-black/

Jan Springer Website at http://www.janspringer.com[1]

Instagram – http://www.instagram.com/janspringerauthor

Facebook - https://www.facebook.com/janspringereroticromance

Jan's Blog - http://janspringerauthor.wordpress.com/blog-2/

Happy Reading,

                Jasmine Black / Jan Springer

---

1.   http://www.janspringer.com/

Don't miss out!

Visit the website below and you can sign up to receive emails whenever Jan Springer publishes a new book. There's no charge and no obligation.

https://books2read.com/r/B-A-WGQ-OJNGG

BOOKS 2 READ

Connecting independent readers to independent writers.